A Family of Strangers

Casey S. Bell

Library of Congress

Cover Design: CSB Design and Printing

Published by: BookCase Publishing

Editor: Michael Valentine

Printed in USA

CONTENTS

CHAPTER ONE

No one ever knows the day that will detour their path. These detours are not always bad, but they are unexpected changes that bring fear, nerves, and uncertainty. However, if one follows, it reveals a side of themselves they were unaware existed.

William Osei is a twenty-five-year old family service specialist, a handsome man, six feet tall and an athletic body type, single and not ready to settle down. He is in his office at Bambin Adoption and Foster Agency or sometimes referred to as BAAFA; he has been working for three years a monotonous schedule from nine to five and five days a week. Today he is at his desk organizing and filing paperwork. As he works, the phone rings. William answers. "Aamir, I'll never get any work done if you keep calling me."

Aamir says, "Sorry William. There's a couple out here who would like to speak to you. Their names are Matthew and Margaret Smith."

William mumbles to himself, "What do they want now?" Speaking to Aamir, he says, "Let them in please, thank you."

The door opens and a man enters, behind him walks his wife, and behind her walks a ten-year-old boy, Bobby Sampson. He has red hair, and green eyes. He stands behind Matthew with fear. Matthew speaks. "We need to talk to you about something."

William says, "Mr. and Mrs. Smith, what a pleasure to see you. How is everything? Where's Bobby?"

Matthew turns to look for Bobby; he steps away and notices Bobby is right behind him. William walks towards Bobby. "There you are; why are you hiding?"

Matthew glares at William. "We need to talk, now."

William walks to his desk and calls Aamir on the intercom. "Aamir, come here please."

William approaches the Smiths. "So, Matthew, how's the job?"

Matthew answers, "We're not here to talk about my job."

Aamir enters the room.

"Oh, Aamir, can you show Bobby where the playroom is?"

"Sure."

Aamir beckons to Bobby. "Come on, Bobby, come with me, I am going to show you one of the best playrooms this world has to offer."

Aamir and Bobby leave the office. William closes the door, and then he sits at his desk.

"So, how may I help you Mr. and Mrs. Smith? What's on your mind? You look disturbed."

William goes through more paperwork, Margaret walks towards his desk and slams her purse on the desk. William, stunned, looks up at her. She says, "Can't you do that at another time, we're trying to have a meeting with you. We need your undivided attention."

William responds attentively, "I'm sorry. How may I help you?"

Matthew speaks. "You can start by taking him back."

William's eyes widen. "What do you mean? I thought you guys were getting along."

"Well, you thought wrong," Matthew counters. "He's not responding to us."

"What do you mean he's not responding to you?"

"Exactly what he just said," says Margaret, "he doesn't respond, we ask questions, and he doesn't respond, he barely speaks, it's like he's afraid of us. What are we supposed to do?"

"It takes time. Do you know how many people have quit on him? He doesn't talk, because he's uncomfortable, he's not sure whether or not he's going to be moved. He has been here since birth, and has been in at least twenty homes, and he's only ten years old. It's rough on him, just give it another month," William says.

"We can't. I don't think I have the energy or the patience."

William walks towards Matthew. "Do you know what Bobby is thinking?"

Matthew shakes his head no.

"He's thinking that you are going to give him up like every other family. You cannot give up on him. He needs a stable home."

Margaret says, "Well, it's not our home. Sorry, William, but we don't want him."

William walks to his desk. "Well, what am I supposed to tell him?"

Matthew says, "That's your problem. We've done all we could do with him."

Margaret speaks. "There's nothing more we can do, William. We're really sorry."

Matthew takes his wife's hand and walks towards the door. As they exit William stops them. "Wait a second."

Matthew responds in anger, "Just forget it, we've made our decision, and you can't change it."

William picks up Margaret's purse.

"You're forgetting something."

Margaret walks over to William and takes her purse, and then she looks at him straight in the eye, "I'm sorry, William, we really tried, but nothing worked." She walks towards her husband and they exit the office.

William sits at his desk. "What am I supposed to do?"

William calls for Aamir on the intercom. "Aamir, are you there?"

"Yes William."

"Come in, please."

"Yes, William."

William begins to look for Bobby's paperwork; as he does Aamir walks in. "William, you called for me?"

"Yes. Did you see the couple that just left this office?"

Aamir nods his head yes.

"They are the worst couple in the world, Matthew and Margaret Smith. I want you to get that name in your head, so the next time you hear it you know that they are the world's best quitters."

Aamir cocks his head. "Why are you so angry?"

"They walked out on Bobby. They said they didn't want him anymore. They returned him like he was a damaged product. Does this office look like the return line at a department store?"

William stands. "What am I supposed to do? What am I supposed to tell Bobby?"

Aamir answers, "Tell him the truth, there is no need lying to him."

William walks towards Aamir. "You can't be serious; I can't tell a ten-year old his foster parents dropped him off because they didn't want him anymore. He already thinks badly of himself. Do you know how many houses he has lived in?"

Aamir responds, "No I don't, but that doesn't matter. The truth is always better than a lie."

William sits at his desk. "But what do I say? I don't want him to feel badly. Besides, he needs a home to live in. He's been back and forth all his life."

Aamir walks towards William's desk. "I understand, but there's nothing you can do, but put him back into foster care and hope another family takes him."

William snaps, "No, I cannot do that; no child should go through that. I have to think of something else."

Aamir stares at William. William responds, "Why are you staring at me like that?"

Aamir replies, "It's nothing, I was just thinking of something."

"What were you thinking?"

"I was thinking...well, since you're so worried about him, you adopt him? He'll have a permanent home. Besides, he sees you every time a family brings him back to this office, he knows you."

William stands. "Me, being a father, I don't think that would work."

Aamir responds, "Then you obviously don't want to help him."

William walks towards him. "That's not true; I want to make sure he grows up feeling good about himself, but I can't take him home."

Aamir walks towards the door. "I'm going to bring Bobby in here. You have a choice, you can tell him he has to live in foster care, because the Smiths gave up on him, or you can tell him he's going home with you. I hope you make the right decision. You can be the one who makes a change in this boy's life."

William is in his room dressing. After he is done he gets his briefcase, leaves his room and walks past the bathroom door, stops, and returns to the door. He knocks on the door and there is no response, he knocks again, no response. William knocks again and then asks, "Bobby, are you alright?"

Bobby opens the door and nods his head yes at William.

"Okay, when you're done come to the kitchen, okay?"

Bobby nods his head yes. William walks downstairs into the kitchen and sets his briefcase near the counter. He opens the refrigerator door and takes two bagged lunches and places them next to his briefcase. He then gets two bowls and spoons and sets them on the kitchen table.

He opens the cabinet and fetches a box of cereal and oat milk from the refrigerator. He walks towards the table and makes two bowls of cereal. As he does so, Bobby walks downstairs and into the kitchen. William notices him and says, "There he is, the best boy in town."

Bobby doesn't respond.

"Would you like some cereal?"

Bobby sits at the table and eats. William smiles and sits next to him and eats.

"So, I see you like fruit rings. I like them too. So, how's school going...are the teachers and students treating you well...did you make any friends yet? Well, don't worry; you'll make some friends soon. I remember my first day of school. I was so afraid of everything, but once I got comfortable all my fears went away."

Bobby continues to eat; he looks up at William every now and then without responding.

"So, are you ready to go to school?"

Bobby looks up and shrugs. William takes the bowls of cereal and puts them in the sink. He then takes his briefcase and the lunch bags.

"Come on, partner, let's go."

BAMBIN ADOPTION AND FOSTER AGENCY OFFICE

William is sitting at his desk in front of a computer, typing. Aamir enters and asks, "Hey William, how's Bobby coming along?"

"Well, it could be better. This morning I was talking to him and he never responded to me. I spoke and he listened, he never said a word. Well, except when I asked him if he was ready to leave."

Aamir smiles. "What did he say?"

"He said I don't know."

Aamir gets excited. "Well, at least he spoke to you."

William frowns. "He didn't talk; he shrugged his shoulders. But, I know one of these days...I'm not giving up on him. I am going to make sure I take care of him."

Aamir smiles. "I'm glad. He needs a father like you."

William seems shocked. "Father? I'm not sure I feel comfortable being called a father."

Aamir says, "Well, if you plan on keeping him until he's eighteen, I'm sure he'll start calling you dad. Well, unless his parents return."

William laughs. "That'll never happen, last I heard his parents are long gone, and don't care for him. Isn't that sad?"

"Yes, it's very sad, but with you around I believe everything will work out for the best. You know, sometimes God gives us blessings, but because they are not what we think they should be, we miss them."

William smiles. "Well, I'll make sure not to miss this one. I am going to take good care of my blessing. I just hope my blessing starts speaking to me."

Aamir replies, "Give it some time. I'm sure he'll come around, patience is the key to life."

William smiles and walks towards Aamir. "Would you like a podium, preacher?"

Aamir replies, "Is that supposed to be a joke?"

"Wow, you're quick."

"Oh, so you got jokes?"

They laugh; a knock is heard at the door, and William opens it. On the other side is a young light brown skinned woman with beautiful black hair and a purple business suit.

"Hello, Patricia, how's the best boss in the world doing?"

Patricia responds, "Why are you sucking up to me?"

"Me suck up? I never suck up."

Aamir laughs at William's response. "Good morning, Patricia."

"Good morning, Aamir, nice to see you again."

"William, I need to speak with you."

William looks at Aamir and then at the door. Aamir says, "I'll see you later; I have to get back to work."

William sits at his desk. "So what did you need to talk about?"

Patricia sits on a chair next to his desk. "I overheard you adopted a little boy."

"Yes I did, his name is Bobby Sampson. I felt like I had to. His last parents dropped him off like he was a defective device."

Patricia smiles at the comment. "Well, you know it happens all the time around here. It is not the first time; sometimes the children just don't behave."

"I promise you, Bobby is not as bad as they made him seem. He just doesn't talk, which is understandable."

William stands in anger. "I mean he's been from house to house all his life."

Patricia responds,

"You don't have to explain it to me, I completely understand."

William sits. "I just which the Smiths understood. Well, how did you know I adopted him?"

"Aamir was talking about it to everyone. I had to come in to ask if it was true. You know, that was a big step, I'm proud of you. Don't think about the Smiths, they gave up a blessing. Besides, they would have been a burden to him; I'm glad you adopted him. He needs a good home and I know you can provide that for him."

Patricia stands. "I know you'll be good for him. I'll see you tomorrow; I have a lot of things that need to be done before five o'clock."

Patricia leaves the office. William sits down at his desk and continues to work with a smile on his face.

"Patricia is right, I am good for Bobby. I will have him talking in no time."

SUPERMARKET

William is walking down the aisle pushing a basket; Bobby is walking by his side. William is reviewing a shopping list in his hand. William and Bobby walk around the supermarket for a while before William walks towards the register.

"Bobby, would you like anything?"

Bobby looks at William and nods no.

"Are you sure, I can get you whatever you want: cereal, cookies, candy, whatever you want."

Bobby quietly says, "No thank you."

William smiles. "Okay, but whenever you need anything don't be afraid to ask."

As they walk toward the check-out aisle, a mysterious woman follows them. Neither William nor Bobby notices her. She stands behind them in the checkout. She watches them as they buy their items. There is a glow about her that lets you know she is relieved and happy. As they leave, the sales associate tries to get her attention. "Ma'am, excuse ma'am; May I help you?"

The woman says, "Oh, um, no. I'm sorry."

The woman leaves the supermarket.

The doorbell rings twice. William runs downstairs and goes to the door and opens it. Standing there is a distinguished, wealthy, and youthful woman. As the door opens, William's eyes open wide in shock. "Mother, what are you doing here?"

"Thanks for offering me to come in."

"Oh, I'm sorry, Mom, come in. It's just a shock to see you here. Usually you call before coming."

"Yes, that's true, but today is a different day, I thought I'd come unannounced."

Edna walks towards the living room; William closes the door and follows her.

"Is there something wrong; how's father doing?"

"Everything is fine, including your Father. I came to ask some questions. You will never believe what I heard from your neighbor, Gloria."

Edna sits on a love seat, William sits on the couch across from her, and he answers, "What has she gossiped about me now?"

"Aren't you going to offer me refreshment?"

William stands. "Oh, right, I'm sorry; would you like a drink or something to eat?"

"No, thank you, I'm fine."

William sits down. "Well, what did she say?"

"She said you adopted a son. Once I heard I told her that it isn't true, but she assured me it was, so I came here to find out for myself."

William says, "Well, she's right; his name is Bobby",

Edna interrupts him. "What do you mean? You can't be serious."

"Mother, I am very serious."

"Why would you adopt a son, you're not even married."

"I know, Mother, it just happened, it wasn't planned."

Edna sits next to William. "I don't understand. You mean to tell me you adopted a son unplanned. Please explain this to me."

William replies, "He was one of my children at the office. No one wanted him. About two weeks ago he was dropped off by his foster parents. It was his twenty-something house that he lived in, and he's only ten years old. I didn't have the heart to tell him his foster parents didn't want him, so I took him home. At the time it was the only reasonable thing to do."

"Are you sure it was a good thing to do? I mean twenty-something homes; obviously this child is nothing but trouble."

William answers quickly, "Not necessarily, the only complaint I've received is that he doesn't speak much, which is understandable. He's been in foster home after foster home, and he's never met his biological parents. That's a lot for a child to handle."

Edna says, "Well, how are you doing with him?"

William stands and walks behind the couch. "Not so well, he doesn't talk to me either and he never knows what he wants, but he'll come around."

Edna shakes her head. "I don't know, son. You know your father is going to be so surprised when I tell him."

There is a silence before Edna asks, "Well, where is this boy?"

William smiles and responds quickly, "You want to meet him?"

"Well, yes, I guess."

"You're going to love him, Mom."

William runs upstairs. A few seconds later, William walks downstairs, Bobby follows him. They both walk towards the living room. As they walk towards the living room, Edna stands. William walks towards Edna.

"Bobby, I want you to meet someone. This is my mother."

Timidly, Bobby stands next to William. Edna walks toward Bobby; she puts her hand out. "Hello, Bobby, it's nice to meet you."

Bobby continues to stand next to William, William directs him to Edna. "Say hello to Grandma Edna."

"William, I am not that old. You may call me Edna."

Bobby doesn't respond. Edna says, "What's wrong, honey; cat's got your tongue?"

Bobby shrugs his shoulder.

Edna laughs. "You're right, William, he's adorable, and look at that hair and his eyes, they're beautiful. Well, it was nice meeting you, Bobby. William, I hope you know what you're doing. I'll see you later, son."

William kisses her.

"Bye, Mother, thanks for stopping by."

"Oh, it was no problem, I enjoy coming to see my son, stay in touch."

Edna walks towards the door, William follows her. As they walk towards the door, William turns around and winks at Bobby. He continues towards the door and opens it for Edna,

"Thanks, son, see you later. Bye, Bobby."

She exits, William closes the door. William walks towards Bobby.

"Don't be afraid of her, she doesn't bite."

William walks towards the living room and sits, Bobby follows him.

"You don't have to fear her. I was never afraid of her." William pauses and thinks.

"Well, there was only one time when I was afraid of my mother."

Bobby, interested, asks, "What happened?"

William is shocked by his response smiles, and then he continues, "Well, I was playing with a baseball in the house. She always told me not to, but this one time I did. I was in my room trying to aim at a target, but the ball went through my window. When she heard the window break she ran upstairs to see what happened. Once she found out what happened she was so upset, I think I saw smoke coming out of her ears."

Bobby smiles at his comment, William responds with a bigger smile.

"My parents were so upset, because they knew it would cost a fortune to get the window fixed. To pay for it I had to do the laundry, dishes and mow the lawn for three whole months. I was upset for days, but I never played in the house again."

Bobby, even more interested now, asks, "Do you still play baseball?"

William smiles. "Well, not really. With work there's not much time, besides I have no one to play with. It's pretty difficult to play baseball by yourself."

Bobby says, "I play at school at recess. It's so much fun."

William asks, "Are you any good?"

"Ritchie says I am. He says that I should join the little league."

William is amazed that Bobby is speaking

"Who is Ritchie?"

"He's this boy at school. He asked me if I would be his friend, and now we do everything together."

William becomes more excited at each response from Bobby.

"You have friends? Do you talk in school?"

Bobby smiles. "Well, I didn't at first. I was kinda scared, but after Ritchie became my friend his friends became my friends. He has nice friends."

William laughs. "This is amazing. So, you really like baseball?"

Bobby smiles. "Yes I do, I want to join the Little League team Ritchie keeps talking about, but I was afraid to ask you."

William responds, "Why? You don't have to be afraid to ask me anything. If you really want to try-out for the team, we can do that. The first thing we have to do is go to a sports store and get you some baseball gear, a glove, and a bat, so we can practice."

Bobby says, "We're going to need a ball too."

"Of course, how could I forget, the ball. We're going to get a ball and all that other stuff so you will be ready to try-out for the Little League."

Bobby smiles. "Thank you, William."

William responds, "You're welcome, Bobby. I want you to know, whenever you need or want something don't be afraid to ask. So, tell me more about Ritchie and your friends."

BAMBIN ADOPTION AND FOSTER AGENCY OFFICE

William is sitting at his desk writing. Aamir enters with papers.

"William, these have to be signed."

William responds, "How soon do they need to be signed?"

Aamir answers, "They need to be signed two days from now. I need to mail them by then."

"Then just place them on top of the pile."

There is a pile of papers on the right side of William's desk. Aamir looks at the pile, and then places the papers on top. Aamir says sarcastically, "What is this, your, I'll get to it before next year pile?"

William says, "No, I just have a lot of work to do, this is my, it can wait pile. The pile over here is the pile that needs to be done right away."

Aamir looks at the pile. "You mean the pile on the left."

William nods yes.

Aamir says, "That's a small pile. Have you heard of the word procrastination?"

William responds, "I am not procrastinating; I'm just doing the most important work first."

Aamir changes the subject. "So, how are things with Bobby?"

William stops working and stands. "I am so glad you asked; it's going great."

Aamir responds, "Oh, really, is he talking?"

William laughs. "He doesn't stop. We talk about everything, sports, television, food...girls."

Aamir interrupts. "Girls? Isn't he a bit young to talk about girls?"

"I don't know; all I do know is that he asks questions. He has a crush on this girl at school."

Aamir smiles at William's last comment. William continues, "Don't you remember your first crush? Mine was Robin Singapore, in the fourth grade."

Aamir says, "That's cute."

William sits. "Last week he tried-out for Little League and he made the team. I am so proud of him, each day I feel like he is more and more my son. I had so much fun practicing with him, and when he made the team it made me even happier."

"Well, I am happy for you, with you, I am happy with you."

"Thank you, Aamir."

"No, problem, well, I need to get back to work, I will be at my desk."

As Aamir leaves the office Patricia enters. "Hi guys," she says, and then she notices the pile. "What's the mountain for?"

William responds, "Just some work that needs to get done."

Patricia says, "I came to get the papers for the Wilson case; I hope you can find it amongst these papers."

William walks to his desk. "Oh, I have them ready." He goes in his desk to get a folder. "Here they are, all packed and ready to go."

Patricia takes the folder. "Thanks, William. So, how are things with Bobby?"

William smiles. "Things are going great. Bobby is finally warming up to me."

Patricia smiles. "I told you things would be okay. I only wish the best for you and Bobby."

William says, "Oh, would you like to come see him play?"

Patricia asks, "Play what?"

William answers, "He's in Little League baseball. It's this Saturday; his first game."

"Oh, I don't know, I was planning on relaxing. Besides, I don't know that I want to be around a bunch of ten year olds and their competitive parents."

Williams promises, "It won't be that bad."

"I'm really not sure."

As she talks Aamir reenters the office with papers. "William, more papers to sign."

William takes the papers and places them on the pile. "Aamir would you like to come to Bobby's first Little League game?"

Aamir, excited, answers, "Of course I would, thanks for asking."

William says, "See, Patricia, Aamir is excited to go. How bad can it be?"

Patricia hesitantly says, "I'll think about it. Well, I'll see you later."

LITTLE LEAGUE BASEBALL FIELD

It is a sunny Saturday morning; the out of control children, competitive parents, hot dogs, and lemonade all share a spot at the Little League baseball field. The game is on its last inning. It is like any other Little League game, over-excited children, and their parents who don't understand the concept of fun and games. William, Aamir, and Patricia are sitting in the bleachers.

Yells of parental encouragement fill the place.

"Come on Samuel you can do it!"

"That's my boy, go on Linell hit that ball out of the park."

"Pitch it real good, Jeriahel."

"Zyyihr, get ready to run home."

Patricia looks at William. "You see what I mean, William, this place is full of parents who don't know how to teach their children that setting goals and reaching them is more important than winning a silly baseball game. If a fight breaks out, I'm leaving."

William says, "Don't worry; nothing bad is going to happen."

A couple approaches William, the woman says, "Hello, William."

Williams says, "Carla and Richard how are you?"

Carla responds, "We're doing well. We would have come over earlier, but we saw you had people with you and we didn't want to impose. Do you mind introducing us to your friends?"

"Oh my gosh, where are my manners? I'm sorry, Carla, Richard this is my boss Patricia Chang and this is my assistant Aamir Sultan." They all shake each other's hands.

Williams turns his attention to Patricia and Aamir. This is Richard and Carla Santiago, Ritchie's parents."

Patricia says, "Should we know Ritchie?"

William responds, "Oh, I'm sorry; Ritchie is Bobby's best friend. I thought I mentioned that."

Patricia and Aamir shake their heads no.

William says, "Oh, sorry."

Richard speaks. "Do you mind if we sit with you?"

"Oh, no, of course not."

Carla says, "So, Patricia, Aamir, how long have you worked for Bambin Adoption and Foster Agency?"

Patricia answers, "I worked for BAAFA for fifteen years, and I've been William's boss for ten of them."

William says, "She is the best boss an employee can have."

Carla smiles and continues, "What about you, Aamir?"

"I've worked for William for six years."

Carla continues, "It must be sad to work around all those parentless children."

Patricia says, "It is. Everyday I do my best to make sure at least two children are adopted. It makes a difference."

Carla answers, "I know what you mean, when William told us about Bobby, I thought, what a great man he is."

"We all thought that," says Amir, He made a good choice by adopting him."

Carla says, "That's exactly what I thought. Richard, what you do you think?"

"I think Ritchie better hit this one out of the park if he wants to come home."

"Honey, is all you can think about is winning this silly game?"

"It's not a silly game. Their pitcher is really good; if they want to win they have to get a home run."

Patricia mumbles to William, "You see what I mean."

Richard yells, "Come on, Ritchie, hit it out of the park."

A man yells back, "Not a chance."

Richard calls, "How 'bout you keep your mouth shut."

The man replies, "Come over here and shut it."

Richard starts to walk over to the man when Carla stops him. "Richard, ignore him, this is not about us it's about the children."

Patricia looks at William, William says, "Nothing is going to happen."

Everyone goes back to watching the game. The pitcher pitches the ball and Ritchie swings. "Strike one!"

Richard yells, "Ah, come on, that's the pitcher's fault!"

The pitcher pitches again and Ritchie hits it.

Richard yells, "That's my boy, run all the way home."

The crowd is responding to the hit. Richard, Aamir, and William are standing and cheering Ritchie on. Ritchie runs to first base and stays. The coach yells, "Stay, don't run."

Carla stands. "That's my boy."

They all sit down; William says to Patricia, "See, isn't this fun?"

"I guess it is, if you like screaming."

"Come on, Aviyah" yells a woman.

Aviyah goes to bat. The pitcher pitches he hits it and runs towards first base. His parents stand and yell, "Run Aviyah. Run!" The other parents cheer him on. Ritchie gets to second base and stops.

"When does Bobby go up?" asks Aamir.

"I'm not sure," says William.

A man stands up as a boy walks to the batting area.

"That's my boy, Kaeden, make me proud."

The pitcher pitches, Kaeden hits the ball and runs to first base, the pitcher catches the ball and throws it to first base. Kaeden slides onto first base. "Safe!" yells the umpire.

"That's my boy," yells his dad.

Kaeden stands up begins to dust off his uniform, his mother says, "Thank God for bleach."

The other mothers laugh at her comment. Bobby walks towards the batting area. William smiles and stands, yelling "Hit it out of the park, Bobby."

Aamir stands. "Show that pitcher who's he messing with."

Patricia looks at both of them and then nods her head. "I don't believe you two."

The pitcher pitches the ball, and Bobby swings. "Strike one."

"That's okay, Bobby, you can do it," yells William.

The pitcher pitches again and Bobby swings and misses again.

"Come on, Bobby you can do it," yells Aamir.

"I don't like that pitcher," says Carla.

Richard says, "That's okay, Bobby can hit it, that pitcher is no threat." The pitcher pitches again Bobby hits it out of the park.

"Oh my gosh," says William.

Patricia in amazement stands and watches as the ball flies. Bobby and the rest of his teammates run home. The crowd cheers.

Patricia says, "Wow, William, he's good."

William responds, "I know... I know."

As the boys run home and the game ends the parents leave the bleachers as the players come to the bleachers.

"He won his first game," says William.

"I am so proud of my son," William says to Richard.

"You guys want to come over my house? I'm having a party for Bobby to celebrate his first game. I know he would love it if Ritchie was there."

Richard says, "How did you know he was going to win?"

"I didn't, I was going to have it whether he won or lost."

Carla says, "Oh that's so sweet. We would be delighted to come."

Richard says, "Why don't you invite the whole team?"

Carla says, "Richard, he can't have the whole team and their parents at his house."

"Why not?"

"Because that's too many people."

"No it's not. William, is it too many people?"

William hesitantly says, "I guess not."

"No, of course it isn't," says Richard.

Richard yells, "Party for the winning team at Williams's house."

The parents cheer.

"How do we get to his house?" asks a parent.

Richard yells, "Follow me. To the cars."

The children run to their parents. Ritchie and Bobby run towards Richard and William.

Richard says, "There's my boy, you did a great job out there."

William says, "He sure did, both of you did. You continue to play like that and you guys can win every game."

Richard agrees. "That's right, but now it's time to party. William is having a party at his house. So it's time to go."

Ritchie asks, "Can Bobby ride with us, Dad?"

"Of course he can, if his dad say's it's alright."

Williams nods.

Richard says, "Okay, let's go to the car. Last one there is a rotten egg."

Richard, Ritchie, and Bobby run off the bleachers and towards the parking lot. As they run off Carla says, "We'll see you there. It was nice meeting you Patricia."

"Thank you, it was nice meeting you too."

Carla leaves. The parents and crowd begin to leave the park. William asks Patricia, "Are you coming?"

"Coming where?"

"Are you coming to the party?"

Patricia says, "Oh, I don't know."

"Why not? Didn't you have fun at the game? The party will be just as fun."

Patricia thinks for a second. "I can't stay long."

William smiles. "You can follow me home. What about you, Aamir?"

"Sure, why not?"

"Good answer," says William.

William, Patricia, and Aamir walk to the parking lot and leave to William's house.

CHAPTER TWO

WILLIAM'S OFFICE

William is pacing in his office. On his desk is the same pile of papers. As he paces, Aamir enters the office with papers.

"That was a great party on Saturday."

William continues to pace without responding. Aamir continues, "William is there something wrong?"

William continues to pace he begins to mumble to himself. Aamir confusingly asks, "Would you like me to leave?"

William's mumbles get louder and louder. William asks himself, *How could she do this, what was she thinking?*

Aamir is confused. "William...William, William!"

William looks at Aamir. "Oh, hi, Aamir. When did you get here?"

Aamir says, "A couple of minutes ago. You were mumbling to yourself, you're obviously in outer space or somewhere else, but definitely not here. Are you okay?"

William says, "Sure...of course. Everything is just fine."

Referring to the papers in Aamir's hand, he asks "What do you have there?"

Aamir replies, "Oh, just more files to look at. I'll just put them here."

He places them on the pile.

"Thank you," says William.

William at this point is still pacing. There is something bothering him that is unknown to Aamir.

"Are you sure you're okay? You seem worried about something. Is there anything I can do?"

William answers, "No. There's nothing you can do, because there's nothing wrong. I'm okay, I promise."

"Alright, if that's what you say," replies Aamir, "I'll be at my desk if you need anything."

Aamir begins to exit when William calls, "Aamir, I have a question for you."

Aamir looks at William ready to answer.

"Do you think Bobby needs a mother?" Aamir asks.

"What do you mean?"

"You know what I mean. The nuclear family...stuff. They say the best family is a husband, wife and children. I have a child, so it means I need to get married. Right?"

Aamir replies, "Not necessarily. These days there are many types of families."

William continues, "Well, do you think he should have...like...a surrogate mother."

Aamir says, "Not at all, I think you're doing a great job raising him. However, if you think he needs one, I'm sure Patricia wouldn't mind being one."

"Are you crazy, Aamir? I can't ask my boss to be a surrogate mother," says William.

Aamir says, "Well, what about Carla? She baby-sits for him anyways."

William says, "Yeah, but she has a family. I don't know, I just think he needs some kind of a woman figure in his life."

Aamir suggests, "What about your mom?"

"My mother is done with raising children. Besides I don't think I would be able to raise Bobby with my mother."

Aamir asks, "Why all of a sudden the concern for a mother?"

William thinks, I really can't...I mean I know, but I can't...it's not that you won't understand it's just that; I can't tell you. It just came to me after a disturbing phone call.

Aamir is concerned. "When did you get the call? Who was it...what did they say?"

"I really must not talk about it right now. It's just so amazing how things happen. You know how you think some things will never happen. You know, there is no way in hell that it could happen. And then heaven opens its skies and it happens. Well, that's what happened. The one thing I thought that would never happen...it happened."

Aamir confused, asks, "What are you talking about? What happened?" William shakes his head,

"I really mustn't tell you, but I'm sure you'll find out at some point."

Aamir says, "So then why don't you just tell me?"

"I can't."

"Well, whenever you're ready to talk, you know how to reach me."

"Thanks, Aamir. You're a real friend, you're like the nice brother I never had."

Aamir confused, says, "Don't you have an older brother?"

William smiles. "Yes, but he wasn't nice to me."

They both laugh. Aamir says, "Well, I'll be at my desk if you need me."

Aamir walks towards the door and opens it. When he opens it he sees Patricia on the other side about to knock.

She says, "Hey, how did you know I was about to knock? Do you have ESP?"

Aamir replies, "No, but I have ESPN."

They both laugh as Aamir leaves. William is pacing, Patricia notices him. She looks at the piles of paper. "You know, you could get a lot more work done if you spent less time pacing."

William doesn't notice her.

"William...William...William!"

She stomps twice. "Wake up."

William replies, "Oh, I'm sorry, I didn't even notice you. When did you come in?"

William looks around the office, "Where did Aamir go?"

Patricia looks confused. "He left as I walked in. Is there something wrong?"

William is still in outer space. "No, nothing at all. I have a question to ask. Do you think Bobby needs a mother?"

Patricia replies, "Are you thinking about getting married?"

"No. I was just asking."

"Do you think he needs a mother?"

"Well, I guess. I've just been thinking about it lately. You know a child having a mom and dad. I just thought that maybe he could experience what his friends have. I mean he always had two parents, but it always lasted for about a month before they brought him back."

Patricia says, "Yes, that's true, but I think you're doing just fine raising him by yourself. I think when you finally find the right woman she'll understand of your situation."

William says, "You really think so?"

"Yes I do. Don't worry about that stuff now. You have more than enough to think about. Like that pile."

William smiles. "Oh, that'll all be done before the week is out."

Patricia says, "I sure hope so. I think you should go home early today. I think you need rest, you're not yourself today. Go home and relax."

William says, "No, it won't make a difference, I have a meeting at seven tonight."

Patricia says, "Well, it's three o'clock right now. If you go home now it will leave at least three hours to rest. Plus, you won't have to worry about rush hour traffic. Besides, you're not getting any work done. You're just pacing back and forth."

William is pacing as she is talking.

"Stop pacing."

William stops. "I'm sorry, I can't help it."

Patricia says, "Go home and relax. I'll see you tomorrow morning. I hope you'll be feeling better."

Patricia leaves the office. William takes his things and leaves the office in a rush.

JOSALIE WILLIE RESTAURANT

William is sitting in a booth of the Josalie Willie restaurant, as he sits nervously waiting, a woman enters the restaurant. She has brown hair, and is wearing blue jeans and a red blouse. She is directed to William's booth by the greeter. She approaches the booth nervously, more so than William. The woman speaks,

"William Osei?"

William looks at her for a minute than says, "Yes, and you must be Sarah Sampson."

"Yes I am. It's nice to meet you."

William says, "Please sit, I've been waiting for a while. I'm so nervous. I've been here since six."

Sarah confused replies, "Why, I thought we set the meeting for seven?"

"We did, I just couldn't wait that long. My boss let me go home early. I got home at three-thirty. I felt like I was waiting for eternity."

Sarah smiles. "I know you're wondering why I called you. Before you judge me I want you to know I didn't want to give up Bobby. And now that I have finally found him I was wondering if we could make up some arrangements for visitation."

"I don't think that is possible. You have no clue what Bobby has been through. If it wasn't for me he would be in foster care for the umpteenth time. He's been in and out of foster homes ever since he was born."

"I can imagine a lot of children go through that."

"That's not true. Many children have parents who decide to keep their offspring. And some children are adopted by loving families and never have to go from foster home to foster home. I don't think we can arrange anything. It was nice meeting you, but I need to go."

Sarah stops him. "Wait, we just got here."

"You just got here. I've been here for an hour."

"Please, just hear me out. You haven't even heard my story. I love Bobby. When I held him in that hospital it was like heaven, considering the circumstances, but I still loved him."

William responds. "Then why did you drop him off at BAAFA. People who love people don't drop them off like products, especially parents who love their children."

"I asked you not to judge me."

"Why not. If you want to visit a little boy, then go adopt one."

Sarah grabs his arm as he leaves. "You know nothing about me, if you would just let me explain."

William hesitates and then sits. "Go ahead I'm listening."

Sarah begins. "Are you really, because it's not the normal story of a mother who puts her child up for adoption. In fact, it wasn't even my choice."

William asks, "How wasn't it your choice?"

Sarah continues, "Well, it started about twenty years ago. I was married to a wonderful man. Well, at least that's what everyone told me. Christopher and Sarah Anderson, we were not a happy couple, but we survived. He was abusive, destructive, a cheat. I can't even believe the many women he was with.

"He was one of those old fashioned men, the kind of man who wanted his wife to be barefoot and serving him. I cooked, cleaned, did his laundry, I would even bring his slippers to him. He was a beer drinker. He loved his beer. Well, one night he ran out of beer, and he wanted one.

I told him that I would do the shopping the next day and he told me that he couldn't wait that long, he wanted his beer now. It was about ten at night. I told him I would get it the next day, and that it was too late to be out at night just to get beer, he slapped me, so, I went out to get him his beer. I got to the store okay, and I brought the beer and then I left the store. I began to walk home with his beer and the worst thing happened to me."

She pauses as she remembers the night. "A man came up to me and asked for all my money, and the beer. I gave him the money, but I couldn't give him the beer."

William asks, "Why not?"

Sarah continues, "Are you crazy; return home without my husband's beer? He would hurt me more than the mugger. Anyway I told him I couldn't do that, and the next thing I know he got very upset. He just attacked me. I didn't think it was bad, because I thought he would just take the beer and run, but he didn't."

Sarah pauses, there is a tear rolling down her face as she continues to tell the story.

"He grabbed me forcefully and threw my skirt over me. That night I regretted wearing a skirt. In fact, I never wore a skirt after that day. After that he tore off my underwear. I couldn't believe what he was doing. I screamed and screamed, but no one heard me.

"Before the night was over I was raped. I couldn't believe it. After he left I couldn't move. I just laid there. The worst thing about it was my husband didn't even care to find me. My mother and sister filed a missing report. When they found me the only thing my husband asked me was: where is the beer. I felt like trash. After about three weeks I started feeling sick, and I had no clue what it was. So, I went to my doctor and she gave me the news. I was pregnant. I didn't know how to tell Chris, he never wanted children. Before we were married he got a vasectomy, so I knew it couldn't be his. I didn't know what to think. I wasn't even thinking of the rape. All I could think is how upset Chris would be. When I finally told him, he didn't speak to me for days. When he finally realized my pregnancy was by rape, he wanted me to get an abortion. I couldn't, so he yelled, and screamed at me for days. He even beat me a couple of times, hoping I would have a miscarriage."

She takes a deep breath. "Then the day came. I remember as if it was today. I went into labor, and I thought that would be the worst day of my life. After I had the baby, I was somewhat relieved. He was so beautiful. It was a bitter sweet moment, sweet because he was a beautiful baby, bitter because of how he came to be, and of course bitter because of Chris. First of all, he had the baby's name changed to my maiden name. He kept telling me it had no right baring his name. He said he didn't want a rape baby having the name of Anderson, but I didn't care, just as long as I could keep him. I named him Robert Anthony. I caressed him every day. I knew who his father was, but that didn't matter to me. And then the worst day of my life arrived. One day Chris took me out on a date. He said he wanted to apologize for how stupid he was acting. He hired a baby sitter from a top agency, so he said. We went out and I actually had fun with him. However, when we came back home...my baby was gone. He wasn't in his room; he was no where in the house. The baby sitter wasn't there either. I tried to call the cops, but Chris assured me everything was okay. About an hour or two later of worrying and constantly trying to call the cops, Chris finally just came out and told me what he did. That baby sitter he hired was not a baby sitter. Instead she was Chris' friend. Chris hired her to get rid of my baby while he took me out. She took Bobby to an adoption agency and got rid of him like he was garbage. There was nothing I could do. I was afraid to do anything, because Chris told me he would kill me if I did. I spent two years with Chris pretending I was okay with everything. Finally, I got the nerves to go to court and get an annulment on terms of infidelity. I was so afraid he was going to hurt me or try to kill me so I moved in with my sister and her husband. About a year later I changed my name back, and ever since then I have been looking for him. I looked everywhere, but I couldn't find the so called baby sitter and Chris was no help. It took me about seven years just to find him..."

She stands and looks at William with an attitude, "And I'm not leaving until I see him."

At this point her face is full with tears. William begins to wipe his tears. "Are you serious?"

Sarah says, "Of course I am. I wouldn't, I couldn't make this up. You know what just forget it. I see you don't care to help me."

She begins to get up; William stops her, "Wait, don't go. Maybe we can work something out, but I don't want to let him know who you are. At least not right away."

Sarah smiles. "That's fine."

William stands to leave, "I hope your story is true, because if you are lying just to see him, you're only hurting yourself."

"No, no, I promise you it's true, I wouldn't lie. Thank you so much. You have no idea how much this means to me."

William says, "You're welcome." He takes a business card out of his pocket, "This is my work address. I'll be there tomorrow."

She looks at the card. "You work for Bambin Adoption and Foster Agency?"

He nods his head. "That's weird, why did you adopt Bobby?"

"Well, he was in my office at least once a month. Parents kept bringing him back. They said he wasn't talking or responding to anyone. My assistant suggested that I adopt him, so I did. I thought it was a bad idea at first, but I am happy that I adopted him."

Sarah shakes his hand. "Thank you so much. This means the world to me. I miss caressing him. I never forgave myself for going out that day. Thank you William."

William is pacing in the office as Aamir enters. Aamir has a pile of papers in his hand.

"How are you William?"

William says, "I'm doing well, thanks for asking. I'm waiting for a lady named Sarah Sampson; if she comes by let her in."

The pile on William's desk is smaller. Williams takes a pile of papers out of his desk and hands them to Aamir.

"Thank you, I'll have these out by today," says Aamir.

"Thank you, Aamir." Aamir exits the office.

William sits down and taps his fingers on the desk, waiting impatiently for Sarah. There is a knock on the door. William stands and fixes his tie waiting for Sarah. He says, "Come in."

He smiles and stands waiting. As he stands the door opens and Patricia comes in. William says, "Oh, it's just you",

Patricia says, "Well, hi to you too."

"Oh, I'm sorry; I'm waiting for someone important to come. I didn't mean to sound…well, you know."

Patricia says, "It's okay. So who's coming to see you?"

"Just some women I met at a restaurant."

"Oh, is it a girlfriend to be?"

William responds, "No, nothing like that. I can't talk about it right now."

Patricia looks at William's desk. "I see you're finally getting some work done

"Yeah, I couldn't get to sleep last night so I decided to do some work."

Patricia says, "You took your work home; since when?"

"Well, I've just had a lot of things to think about that have been bothering me, and the only way to keep it off my mind is to work."

Patricia says, "Well, there's nothing wrong with that. Just make sure it doesn't interfere with your time with Bobby. You need to spend every bit of time you can, with him."

"Yes, I'm aware of that. Don't worry, I make sure I keep some time opened for him," says William.

A buzzer is heard; William walks to his desk. "Yes Aamir."

"She's here, William," says Aamir.

"Let her in, please."

William mumbles, "She's here."

"Who's here?" asks Patricia.

The door opens, Sarah enters the office. William says, "Patricia this is Sarah, Sarah this is my boss, Patricia." Patricia and Sarah shake hands.

Patricia says, "Well, I'll be leaving."

She walks out of William's office. Sarah says, "Hi, how are you?"

"I'm doing fine, thanks for asking."

"Does you boss know who I am?"

"No. No one knows. I am not sure how to tell them yet."

"I understand. This is a nice office."

"Thank you, so what did you want to do?"

Sarah sits at chair next to William's desk. "I don't want to jump back into his life so quickly. However, I would like to see him daily. I want him to know me, and at some point I would like to tell him the truth."

"So what should I tell him when he sees you? I don't know how this is going to work. I can't just tell him, hey Bobby this is your mother, she decided to spend time with you."

Sarah stands. "It doesn't have to be like that. I don't even want you to mention I'm his mother yet. I just want to see him. He's my baby. I already spent ten years out of his life; I can't spend another moment away from him."

William says, "Then what do I tell him?"

"Tell him...I'm your...sister, and when he gets older...I can explain to him who I am and why I left. He's too young for me to tell him the story."

William says, "I understand that, but I'm not going to lie to him."

"That's okay, tell him I'm your friend, we can become friends, then it won't be lying, says Sarah."

"I don't know. It just doesn't seem like it's going to work out."

"Please, you don't understand, I feel like I lost a part of me."

Sarah begins to cry. "I can't spend another moment away from Robert. I need to see him."

William thinks. "How about this, give me a day or two and I will think about it."

"Please. Consider Robert. He is going to want to know who his mother is at some point. He might as well get to know me now."

"I'll think about it."

Sarah says, "Well, take your time, but not too long, I've spent too much time away from him. Please do this for me."

There's a short silence that fills the room. "I'll let myself out."

Sarah walks out of his office. William goes over to his phone and calls Aamir.

"Aamir, can you come in here for a second, I need your opinion about something."

"Yes, William."

William sits down at his desk, as Aamir walks in the office.

"Yes, William, you need something?"

"William stands; do you know who that woman was?" Aamir says,

"Yes, that was Sarah Sampson."

"Yes, but do you know why she was here?"

"To reclaim Bobby?"

"Yes. How did you know that?"

"I guessed. She has the same last name as Bobby. What are you going to do?"

"I'm not sure what to do. She wants to be back in Bobby's life, but she doesn't want to tell him she is his mother."

"Why not?" Aamir asks.

"Well, she doesn't think he would understand; which he wouldn't. She was raped by a stranger and her husband hired someone to take Bobby to an adoption agency while he took her out on a date."

Aamir says, "Damn, that's terrible. Has she decided when she will tell Bobby?"

"No, she has not. She just said that when he gets older. I don't know how she's going to tell him. I still don't know if I'm going to let her back into his life."

Aamir asks, "Why not, she has every right to see her son. Besides it wasn't her fault that she lost Bobby, it's not like she chose to give him up."

"I know, but what will I tell Bobby? How will I explain her to Bobby?"

Aamir says, "Say she's your friend."

"That's the same thing Sarah said. I don't know. It just all seems weird. I was having a good time with him and then his mother pops up. I thought for sure she was long gone."

"I guess she wasn't. Personally, I think it would be good for Bobby. Besides weren't you worried about Bobby not having a female figure around. Here is your perfect chance to get one."

William says, "That worry only came to me after Sarah called me. I wasn't sure if I would meet with her. Then I began to think about maybe it would be good for Bobby, to have a mother, but I wasn't sure it would work. I mean no matter the circumstances, it's difficult to tell a ten-year-old that his real mother has come back. Just to explain why she left him is difficult enough."

"Yes it is, but the only way you'll know if it works or not is to try. I say to let her see him, I'm sure it will only make things better. Hey maybe you'll really like her and you'll marry."

William says, "Don't go that far. Let's just take this one step at a time."

Aamir says, "Just try it, if things go badly let her know that she can't see him any more. However, if things go well, then just maybe Bobby will have that mother figure you've been talking about."

William says, "Maybe you're right. Thanks Aamir for the advice."

"No problem, William. I'll be at my desk if you need me."

Aamir leaves the office. William sits at his desk and dials the phone. He waits as it rings,

"Oh, hello Sarah, this is William. Call me back when you get a chance. I want to talk to you about Bobby and your visits. So, just call me back when you get a chance, thanks...bye."

William is in the living room pacing back and forth. Bobby is in his room playing with Ritchie. The doorbell rings, William jumps at the sound. He rushes to the door and opens it.

"Oh, hi, Carla, come in."

"I'm here to pick up Ritchie."

"Wait here, I'll go get him."

William goes upstairs to get Ritchie. Carla stays downstairs and waits. As she waits a knock is heard at the door. Carla looks at the door and then looks upstairs. The knock occurs again; Carla goes to open it. As Carla opens the door both Carla and Sarah look shocked. Sarah says, "Oh, um…Hi, is this William Osei's house?"

Carla answers, "Yes it is. Is he expecting you?"

"Yes, I'm his friend, Sarah."

They shake hands, "Well, come in, my name is Carla. I'm William's friend too. Well, my husband and I. And our son, Ritchie, plays with Bobby. They're on the Little League together. They get along great. In fact, that's why I'm here, to pick up Ritchie."

While Carla is talking Sarah has a huge smile on her face from the excitement of hearing about Bobby. Carla says, "What's up with the big smile?"

"Oh, nothing...it's just...it's so...I don't know. It's just William told me a lot about Bobby, I can't wait to meet him."

Carla, responds, "Oh he's a great boy."

As William comes downstairs with Ritchie and Bobby, Sarah looks at Bobby with excitement; she begins to hold back tears.

"Sorry for taking so long. When I went upstairs to get Ritchie the room was a huge mess. I helped them clean up." William notices Sarah,

"Oh, I see you two have met."

Carla responds, "Yes we have. Ritchie it's time to go home. It was nice to meet you Sarah. Bye William, bye Bobby."

William, Carla, Bobby, and Ritchie say bye to each other. Carla and Ritchie leave William's house. Bobby goes upstairs,

"Wait Bobby." Bobby stops, William continues, "I want you to meet someone. This is Sarah; she's a good friend of mine."

Bobby walks towards Sarah and says, "Hello Sarah." Sarah smiles and shakes his hand,

"Hi, Bobby. It is nice to meet you."

Bobby looks at William. "William may I watch television in the den?"

"Yes you may, Bobby."

Sarah watches Bobby as he walks to the den.

"Wow, he's so beautiful. Just as beautiful as the day I held him. With those beautiful green eyes and that bright red hair. So, what do you have planned?"

William says, "Well, just like I said, you're a close friend. You are welcomed to come over at anytime. In fact, why don't you watch television with us?"

Sarah says, "I don't know if that's good right now."

"Come on, it's only television, follow me."

Sarah follows William to the den. William says, "Hey Bobby, do you mind if we watch television with you?" Bobby shrugs his shoulders.

William says to Sarah, "Sit here; I'll go get some refreshments."

William walks to the kitchen. Sarah sits down and watches television.

"So, what are you watching?"

Bobby says, "Cartoons."

"How old are you, Bobby?"

"I'm ten years old."

"Wow, ten years old. What grade are you in?"

"I'm in the fifth grade."

"Do you like school?"

"It's okay. Sometimes it's hard, but I get through it."

"Do you have any friends?"

"Yep, I have lots of them, but my best friend is Ritchie. He was the boy that just left."

"You mean Carla's son."

Bobby shakes his head. "William told me about you being in the Little League." Bobby gets excited and stops watching the television.

"Yeah, it's so much fun. One day I hit a home run and the team won. I'm the best. I'm gonna be in the major leagues when I grow up. Hey, you should come see me play."

Sarah says, "Oh, that's sounds great."

William returns with a tray of refreshments.

"Refreshments for everyone?"

William places the tray on a table. Sarah says to William, "I was talking to Bobby and he told me about his baseball games. He invited me to one of his games."

William thinks for a minute. "Well, of course. Why didn't I think of that? You're going to enjoy it. He's a great player."

Sarah says, "Well, I should be going now, thanks again William."

"No problem. Say good bye to Sarah."

Bobby says, "Bye Sarah."

William and Sarah walk towards the door. Sarah says, "So, did you have any specific plans on the visitations?"

"No. I figured once he gets comfortable with you than you can pick him up from school, baby-sit, and whatever else you can do without, well...you know."

Sarah replies, "Yes, of course, I won't tell him yet. I haven't figured out when the right time will be, but I will. For now, I guess we'll just take one day at a time."

William says, "Yes, one day at a time.

Sarah asks, "When is his next ball game? I want to make sure I'm free to come."

"It's next Saturday. You can ride with me if you want. I tell you Sarah he's a great player. Did you ever play baseball?"

"No. I wasn't interested in sports. I was more into fine arts."

William says without thinking, "Well, then he must get his skills from his father."

Stops to think. "I mean...well, what I meant was."

Sarah interrupts, "It's okay. Thanks again, William, you have no idea how much this means to me."

William says, "No problem. See you next Saturday."

Sarah interjects, "Oh, William, is it possible that I can have a picture of him? Maybe like a school picture?"

"Of course." William gets his wallet opens it and takes a picture out.

"You can have this one."

"Are you sure it's okay?"

"Of course, I have plenty of them."

"Thank you."

"You're welcome."

Sarah and William say bye to each other. William opens the door for Sarah and she leaves his home. He shuts the door and says, "I hope I'm doing the right thing."

William is in his office by his desk working. The pile on his desk is much smaller than previously. Aamir opens the office door and comes in.

"Hey, William, here's some more papers for you to sign."

"Just put it on the pile."

Aamir says, "Oh, looks like someone has been working lately."

William smiles at the response. Aamir continues, "So, have you met with Bobby's mother yet?"

William stops working, "Yes I have, and she's a nice lady. It's a shame what happened to her. We're taking it one day at a time. She's coming to see his baseball game on Saturday."

Aamir says, "Oh, that's a great idea. She'll be able to see him more often. You might want to explain her to your neighbors before they get suspicious."

William says, "Carla ran into her last night while she was picking up Ritchie. She thinks Sarah is my friend. I think I'll keep it like that for now."

Aamir asks, "Isn't it kind of difficult to keep this quiet?"

"What am I suppose to do. Bobby is too young to understand this issue. I don't even know if he knows what sex is, let alone rape. I'm waiting for his thirteenth or fourteenth birthday, or maybe I should wait until he is twenty. Hopefully he'll understand by then."

Aamir says, "What are you going to do once he finds out? Are you going to let Sarah take him back?"

William pauses, "I'm not sure. I never thought about that. I'll think about that when the time comes. Right now I'm just thinking about now."

A knock is heard at the door, William says, "Come in."

Patricia enters. "Hello William, Hi Aamir."

They both greet Patricia.

"William do you have anymore paper work for me?"

William takes some papers out of his desk and hands them to Patricia,

"Thank you, William"

Referring to the pile on his desk. "I see someone is finally getting some work done around here."

William says, "Yes, I have. Are you coming on Saturday?"

"No, I can't. I'm going out with my sisters. They're in town so I thought I'd hang with them. Tell Bobby I said good luck."

Patricia leaves the office. Aamir asks William, "Does Patricia know about Sarah?"

"No, but I do plan on telling her. I just hope everything works out. I really started thinking and I truly want Sarah to have another chance with her son."

William, Bobby, and Sarah enter the house laughing. Sarah joyfully says, "I don't believe how much fun that was. Bobby you really are good, three home runs in one game. You are an awesome baseball player."

"Thank you, Sarah. William, can I go over Ritchie's house? His daddy is having a party."

"Of course, we'll all go. Go up stairs and get cleaned up first."

Bobby, all excited runs upstairs, William replies, "Walk please; we don't want you to fall.

"Sorry, William."

Sarah laughs. "Oh, goodness, he is so cute."

"Are you coming to the party?"

"Oh, I'm sorry, William, I can't. I need to get home."

"Oh, please, just for a little while."

"I really can't, maybe next time. William, thank you, for everything, I had so much fun watching him today. I was fighting back tears. I am so happy to know that a man like you has adopted him. No matter what happens I know that Bobby will have the love he needs to grow into a strong man."

Sarah embraces him with a thankful hug. William says, "Sarah, it's no problem. There's no need to thank me."

"I have to. You could have turned me down, but you didn't. I thank God, because I truly believe he answered my prayers. Every night I would pray to God saying, when I find him make sure that he is in a nice stable home. I never wanted him to be a child who never has a family, you know. I was afraid that the agency would have to kick him out at eighteen. I didn't want that, so I prayed, and prayed, and God blessed Bobby with you. You are a life saver, not just for Bobby, but for me. I thank you."

"You're welcome, Sarah."

They hug once more and then Sarah leaves.

"Thanks again, William.

As she leaves Bobby comes downstairs.

"Where's Sarah, isn't she coming with us?"

"No, sorry, Bobby, she had to leave."

"Oh, that's bad. Well, you ready, William?"

"Yes, I am baseball player of the year. Let's go and have some fun."

CHAPTER THREE

Sarah is standing outside a building just staring at it. She is contemplating whether or not to enter. After some time, she finally walks in. She goes through the proper standards to get checked in. She finally gets escorted to a room and sits. She looks around anxiously, both afraid and nervous. Finally, a scruffy man with red disheveled hair appears with a guard. He is un-hand cuffed and is escorted to Sarah. The man sits. Sarah asks, "Are you Sean…Sean Murphy?"

"Yeah. Who are you?"

"You don't remember me?"

"No. Who are you?"

"My name is Sarah. About ten years ago you raped me."

"Lady, if you're coming in here to condemn me; don't waste your time."

"I didn't come here to condemn you."

"Then what do you want?"

She hesitates before answering, "You have a son."

"What?"

"That night; when you raped me; it produced a son."

"So, what do you want, a check? Can't you see I'm in jail? I don't have any money."

"I didn't come here for money. I just thought that you should know. Besides, I don't have him. My ex-husband gave him up for adoption. A nice young man adopted him and is taking good care of him. I just think that every man who has a child on this earth should be aware of his seeds. And you have one. Well, at least one from me."

"So you came here just to tell me I have a son?"

"That's all."

"How do you know it's mine?"

"I saw him recently. He looks exactly like you; same red hair, same green eyes."

There's a short pause between the two of them before Sean breaks it. "You wouldn't happen to have a picture would you?"

Sarah takes out the picture William gave her and shows it to him. The man begins to cry.

"What did I do? He's beautiful."

He hands her back the picture.

"I'm sorry. I am so sorry. I didn't know. Does he know about me?"

"No. He doesn't know about me either."

"You just said you saw him."

"He thinks I'm a friend of the man who adopted him. He doesn't know I'm his mother. I didn't quite know how to explain to him the whole situation. My ex tricked me. He took me out for a date and hired what I thought was a babysitter to get rid of him. He didn't want children and definitely didn't want a rape baby. I haven't the slightest clue if I will ever get the nerves to tell him I am his mother, but for now I'm just his dad's friend. I've been looking for him for the past seven years and I knew once I found him that I would come see you."

"Why?"

"To tell you about your son. I don't want anything from you. I just wanted to give you the knowledge. I also need to tell you that I forgive you."

There is a slight pause before the man breaks it, "Thank you."

"You're pretty polite for a…never mind."

"I'm sorry. I wasn't in my right mind back then. But being in this prison and going to group therapy has straightened me out. I'll be glad when I can get out."

"When do you get out?"

"Not sure yet. I got fifteen years, but I might get out early. It's been ten years already. I might get out in the next two years. And I am really going to better myself, especially for my son. What's his name?"

"Robert Anthony, but we call him Bobby."

"Bobby. My son's name is Bobby."

"Yeah, and he is an awesome baseball player."

"Really?"

"Yes. I went to his last baseball game and he made three home runs."

"That's amazing. It's bitter sweet."

"Why would you say that?"

"I was supposed to be a Major League player. It was a dream of mine and then I...well, you know."

"Do you mind if I ask you a personal question?"

"Depends."

"Why did you do...what you did?"

He takes a deep breath.

"I...I was messed up, I-"

He's interrupted by the guard

"Times up, man."

Sarah interjects, "Just a few more minutes."

"Sorry, lady. You can come back next week."

"Just a little more time, please."

"Lady, you can come back next week. Same time same place, but for now time is up."

Sean asks, "I'll see you next week, right?"

"Of course."

The guard takes Sean. As the guard and Sean leaves Sarah stands and exits the building.

WILLIAM'S HOUSE

Patricia, Sarah, Aamir, Williams, and Bobby enter the house. Patricia says, "You are an excellent baseball player. I should probably get your autograph now. You're not going to forget me when you become an MVP are you?"

"No."

Everyone laughs. Patricia continues,

"Well, I must be heading back home. I'll see you two on Monday. It was nice meeting you Sarah."

Sarah says, "Same here, Patricia."

Aamir speaks. "I better get going too."

Aamir and Patricia leave they all say their good-byes.

William says, "Hey, Bobby, what do you say to me taking you out for a celebration dinner to Golden's Burgers?"

"Yeah!"

"Okay, go upstairs and get cleaned up."

Bobby hurries upstairs to the bathroom. William asks, Sarah "Are you coming?"

"No. I need to get back home. Thanks for the invite though. I greatly appreciate it. And I thank you for all you are doing for me."

"Not a problem. See you later."

"Bye, William."

Patricia enters the room,

"You wanted to see me, William?"

"Yes. I uh, need to tell you something."

"Is everything okay?"

"Yeah, kind of."

"William, what is wrong?"

"I wanted to talk to you about Sarah."

"Oh, Sarah. Are you coming to me for dating advice?"

"No. I don't know how to tell you this, but…you might want to sit down."

"What, why? William, what is it?"

Patricia sits. William continues, "Sarah is Bobby's mother."

Patricia stands. "What? What do you mean?"

"She came in and she introduced herself and asked if I could let her spend time with him."

"Are you crazy!? Ho do you know for sure?"

William thinks for a moment,

"I don't actually know for sure, I just took her for her word."

"And not once you didn't think she was lying?"

"I don't know. Why would anyone lie about being someone's mother?"

"There are many reasons: they're crazy, or they're crooks. Did you not see, Annie? How do you know she's not just trying to steal him for money?"

"I don't know, I just…I didn't think of all that. She just came to me and told me she was his mother and that her ex stole him from her and some other stuff, I don't know…it just seemed legit."

"Is she trying to get him back?"

"No, she said she's not ready to tell him she's his mother."

"Wait, you didn't tell Bobby?"

"No, the story is too…we don't think Bobby is old enough to understand why he was given up."

"Why did she give him up?"

"She didn't. She was raped and she chose to have the baby, but her husband did not want him."

"She's married?"

"Not anymore. Her ex-husband got rid of him."

"How did he manage to do that?"

"He took her out to eat and hired a baby sitter, but she wasn't a baby sitter she was an old friend of his who took Bobby to the adoption agency while they went out to eat. She dropped him off pretending to be his mother so that no one could track the parents."

"Exactly, and without being able to track them for all we know she could have made this up. How do you know she is not trying to steal your son? Have you left him alone with her?"

"Only once. She babysat him and they were still there when I got back."

"And how do you know they will be there the next time? I mean, you put your trust in some strange women's story. You have no clue that this woman is who she says she is. Did you at least do a background check on her? And how do you know the name she gave you is hers? You can't just believe everybody that comes up to you with a sad story. There are many crazy deceitful people out there. How are we supposed to know for sure she is who she says she is?"

"Well, like you said a background check and we can always do a DNA test."

"Well, that's exactly what I am going to do. You need to tell her we need to do a DNA test. And I know you already allowed her to spend time with her son, but by law there are some things we have to set in place. Do you realize you put your job on the line for her?"

"Yes, but I did it for Bobby as well."

"But, what if she is not his mother? Then what?"

"She has the same last name."

"So she says. How do we know she isn't lying about that?"

"Well, we will take the DNA test and then I will go from there."

"I really wish you would have told me about her the moment she showed up. You know how we run things here."

"I'm sorry, Patricia. I just…I guess I wasn't thinking. I let my emotions get the best of me."

"Well, we will take this one day at time. But I need to see her in here immediately."

"Yes, ma'am."

Sarah is sitting at a table waiting. A guard escorts Sean in the room. Sean sees Sarah and smiles; he walks towards her and sits.

"You came back?"

"I said I would."

"How have you been?"

"Good."

"How's Bobby?"

"He's good."

"Does he still---"

"Look. Sorry to interrupt, but I really came back to finish our conversation. I really need to know why you thought it was okay to violate me the way that you did."

"I didn't think it was okay."

"Then why did you do it?"

"I was a messed up child."

"You keep saying that. What do you mean?"

"I was abused by my father; physically, verbally, emotionally, and sexually. When ever he needed sex and my mother wasn't around he'd come to me."

"My goodness, I am so sorry to hear that."

"I started having sex with girls just to prove I wasn't gay. I didn't want to be gay. I was an awkward child in school. If they found out I was gay they would have bullied me even worse then what they did. My first time with a girl was when I was fourteen. Once I started I couldn't stop. By the time I moved out of the house I was hooking up with women left and right. The night that I…she turned me down. I have never been turned down. It messed me up. I went to a bar and drank myself away. And when I left I just saw you and I…I was not thinking correctly. I wanted it and…I'm so sorry. I hated myself for so long. I thought of you and wondered what you made of yourself. I always wanted the chance to do life again. Go to the police and report my dad and get the help I needed then maybe this would have never happened."

"I used to think the same thing. If I had never married that man this would have never happened. If I would have ran away instead run errands for my husband that night this would have never happened. And although this was a terrible thing for the both of us...I look at Bobby and realize I wouldn't want to change a thing."

"But he is the only good thing that has happened out of all of this."

"And sometimes that is all you need...one good thing. He is the silver lining and I much rather focus on the silver lining than the clouds itself. I am really sorry to hear about what happened to you. "Let me suggest you still report your father."

"Why? What's done is done."

"Because if he abused you there's a chance he is still doing it. Most abusers don't stop because you grow up; they stop because they're forced to."

"I'm sorry, Sarah. I really am."

"I know you are. I forgive you, Sean."

"You plan on coming back or is this it?"

"If you would like for me to return then I will do so."

"I would like that very much."

"Next week same time same place."

"Definitely same place; I'm not going anywhere."

They share a laugh. Sarah says, "I'll see you next week."

"See ya, Sarah."

"See ya, Sean."

A guard escorts Sean as Sarah walks away.

William, Patricia, a nurse and Sarah are in William's office. Sarah has her mouth opened while the nurse is swabbing the inside of her mouth. The nurse says, "You can close it now."

Sarah speaks. "Is this really necessary?"

William answers, "Well--"

Patricia interrupts, "Yes. This is procedure. According to the records, Martha Marion is Bobby's mother; so we need to have solid proof that you indeed are his mother."

Sara replies, "That must be the woman who stole him."

William asks the nurse, "How long does this take?"

"It takes anywhere from five to tens days, but can take more. It all depends on how good the samples are and also how many we have working. Our labs are busy, but we will do our best to get it done quickly. Do you have DNA of the child?"

"Yes."

William takes a plastic baggy out of his brief case.

"Is this good. I got it from his comb."

"This is fine. I will call you as soon as the results are in."

Patricia speaks to the nurse. "Thank you, so much. We greatly appreciate it."

"You're welcome. You guys have a great day."

They each thank the nurse as she leaves.

Sarah says, "Oh, these next few days are going to be a wreck."

Patricia asks, "Why? Just as long as you are telling the truth those tests should come back positive."

"I am, but…still. I often wonder maybe I found the wrong child. I mean he looks like the guy who…you know."

William interjects, "Wait a minute. You saw the guy?"

"Yeah. I had to testify against him in court."

"You didn't mention that."

"Well, sorry for not mentioning every little detail. It's not something I'd like to remember."

Patricia says, "Well, I hope he's your son. And if he is we will have to go over some paper work. We as the state have to deal with you as a parent legally. I know William has nicely allowed you to spend time with Bobby, but legally he went about it the wrong way. Well, you have a great day I need to get back to work."

As Patricia leaves the room William and Sarah greet her with good byes. Sarah says, "I'm really nervous. I wish there was a way to make the results come back faster."

"Well, hopefully the results will be good news."

"I sure hope so. William, thank you once again. I am sorry if I almost cost you your job. I in no way wanted to bring confusion or discourse I was just desperate to see my son."

"It's okay. I take full responsibility. It was my choice and I should have chosen differently."

A slight pause enters the room before William speaks. "I was doing some thinking and I thought that sixteen was a good age. It's not too young and not too late."

"What do you mean?"

"Bobby. I was thinking we should tell him on his sixteenth birth anniversary about you. The Truth. Sit him down and tell him the truth."

"Oh, I see."

"Are you okay with that?"

"That should be fine. However, I don't think I will ever be officially ready to tell him. I feel so ashamed."

"Tell the truth and shame the devil."

Sarah smiles. "Yeah. That sounds like a plan. Sixteen. Sixteen it is."

William is sitting at a desk in the den. He is obviously preoccupied with work. Bobby approaches him.

"Excuse me, William."

"Yes, Bobby."

"Am I disturbing you? I don't want to bother you."

"You can never disturb me. What's on your mind?"

"May I ask you a question?"

"Of course. What is it?"

"Is Sarah your girlfriend?"

"No. She's a good friend of mine."

"Well, she sure spends a lot of time with you."

"She doesn't spend time with me she spends time with us."

"She only spends time with me because of you."

"No, she likes spending time with you."

"Why?"

"Because you are an awesome person and don't you ever forget that. Why are you so concerned anyway?"

"I was afraid that if she was your girlfriend and she moved in that you would get rid of me."

"First of all she is not my girlfriend. Secondly, she is not moving in, and lastly, I could never get rid of you. I love you. I adopted you. That means you're my son. Nothing or no one will cause me to get rid of you. Okay?"

"Okay. Uh, William."

"Yes, Bobby."

"Would it be a problem if I started calling you Dad?"

"Not at all, son."

"Okay, Dad. That's all for now. You can get back to work now."

Bobby walks upstairs to his room. William stares with a smile of satisfaction.

Aamir enters the office. "You called, William?"

"Yes. Here is some more paperwork. Can you send those out today?"

"Yes, of course. So you nervous about the tests?"

"I don't know, man. What if Patricia is right? What happens if she is not his mother?"

"She'll probably go to jail."

"But if she does how do I explain her to Bobby? I already told him she was a friend. If she ends up in jail, then he's going to start asking questions. I don't know if I could go through that."

"Well, let's hope she is his mother. If she is, do you have plans to tell Bobby when he gets older?"

"Yes. We agreed on sixteen."

"Sixteen?"

"Yes. On his sixteenth birth anniversary we are going to tell him everything."

"No offense to you man, but I am glad I am not you."

"No, man, its okay. I am sure there is a life lesson in this somewhere."

"Well, when you find it let me know. I'll have these out before the day ends."

"Okay, Aamir. Thanks again."

Patricia is in the office with William having a casual conversation. As they commune Aamir opens the door and allows Sarah in the office. Sarah speaks. "Sorry I'm late. I couldn't sleep a wink last night. When I finally fell asleep the alarm went off. I hit the snooze button and went back to sleep."

Patricia says, "It's okay. Are you ready?"

"Yes I am."

William says, "Good luck."

Patricia continues, "On the matter of Bobby Sampson—Oh my gosh I sound like one of those trashy talk show hosts. On the matter of Bobby Sampson, Sarah, you are his mother."

Sarah exhales as tears come rolling down. Patricia asks, "Are these happy tears or sad tears?"

"Bitter sweet."

Williams in confusion asks, "Why would this be bitter sweet?"

"I can just feel his little heart breaking once I tell him the truth. I don't know that I can ever tell him."

"We agreed on sixteen. His heart won't be little then."

"It doesn't matter if he's fifty. This kind of information would hurt anyone."

Patricia says, "Well, you have six years to strengthen your courage. No matter how terrible the truth; I truly believe the truth is always better than a lie. Well, here are your results you can have these. William did you send out the paperwork yet?"

"Yes. I had Aamir do it"

"Okay. Well, see you later."

Patricia exits the office. William gets tissue and hands it to Sarah. Sarah says, "Thank you."

"It's going to be okay, Sarah. Just take it one day at a time. Let the future take care of itself. You just focus on today."

"Thank you, William. I really appreciate all that you have done."

"No problem."

Sarah has a small photo album and is showing Sean pictures.

"This is him at the baseball field with his friend Ritchie. This is him at Ritchie's birth anniversary party. That was really fun. Ritchie's father sure knows how to throw a party. This is him and his dad; I took them to an opera."

"They agreed to go to an opera?"

"I had to do some teeth pulling, but they went. I think William enjoyed it."

"Thank you, Sarah for doing this. I don't know anyone in your situation who would do this."

"I told you, every father deserves to know if he has a child on earth. And the same goes for you. Not many men in your situation would allow me to do this."

"I'm really sorry, Sarah. I wish there was a way I could pay you back or take it back."

"I've forgiven you. That's all that needs to happen between you and me. It is now time for you to forgive yourself."

"I know. The counselor keeps telling me that, but it is easier said then done."

"Well, focus on that fact that I have forgiven you and not on what you've done to me."

"Thank you, Sarah. This means a lot to me."

"You're welcome, Sean. I shall see you next week."

"Same time same place. See ya, Sarah."

"See you later, Sean."

CHAPTER FOUR

It is two years later and Bobby is twelve years old. He is still playing the best baseball seen in town and is a small town celebrity. He has made the town newspaper a few times. William still works for BAAFA, but has been transitioning. He has thoughts of resigning due to his home-based business. Sarah still spends time with Bobby as well as Sean. Sarah for the last two years has spent her Christmas Eve with Sean and her Christmas Day with William and Bobby. She is excited about her new life, but every now and again gets afraid of the truth. Not the truth about Bobby, but a new arising truth. Sarah has an unexpected meeting today with William. She is aware of it, but not William. She rings the doorbell. William walks to the door.

"Hey, Sarah. Come in. Is everything okay? It's unlike you to come over without calling."

"Is Bobby here?"

"No, sorry. Richard took him and Ritchie to Lenice Jay's Arcade. Is everything okay?"

I'm not sure. I'm glad he's not here. I need to speak to you about something. I am not sure how you are going to take this, but I don't think I should hide it anymore."

"What is it?"

"After I found you and Bobby I sought out Sean Murphy."

"Who is Sean Murphy?"

"He's the man who raped me."

"What? What do you mean?"

"I wanted him to know he had a son. I also wanted to know why he raped me."

"Because he's a pervert. Why would you do something so stupid?"

"Hey, it's not stupid and he's not a pervert. He's a broken person who needs help and he's getting it."

"How do you know?"

"Because every time I see him he's a different person. I can feel he's changing."

"What do you mean every time?"

"Every time I visit him."

"Well how often do you visit him?"

"Once a week."

"WHAT? For how long?"

"For the past two years."

"WHAT? Are you kidding me? Why would you keep visiting him?"

"Because, he's a good man who got messed over as a child. He's getting the help he needs to become a better man. Don't you believe in forgiveness?"

"Well, yeah, but there's a difference between forgiving your rapist and visiting him like he's a family member."

"We share a son together."

"That doesn't mean anything. I don't believe this. And he's okay with your visits?"

"I wouldn't have kept going if he wasn't. He likes our visits. He looks forward to them. No one in his family ever visits him. I am all he has."

"I don't blame them. Who would want to visit a rapist?"

"If you knew his story you would understand."

"He's a rapist."

"He's forgiven. We all are. No sin is less or greater. Who are we to judge?"

"I just don't understand this. Aren't you angry with him?"

"I was, but once he told me his story I now understand him. We were both on the same paths when we met. Both being abused. The only difference is he was aggressive and took his anger out on me; where as I was passive and kept it to myself. I didn't come here to argue with you. I came here for help."

"What kind of help could you need in this situation?"

"Don't jump to conclusions, okay? Just here me out."

"Go ahead, I'm listening."

"I told you about my husband, Right?"

William nods his head yes.

"He was condescending, rude, sexist, a bigot, unloving; he was everything I did not want in a husband. We never had a real conversation, and honestly I don't know how I could have been so dumb to marry him."

"What is your point?"

"There is something about Sean that I like. The time I spend with him I anticipate."

William interrupts, "Please, do not tell me what I think you are about to tell me."

"I can't say that I love him yet, but there is a strong like."

A hard silence hits the room before William breaks it, "How the hell did you fall in love with your rapist? Do you realize how crazy you sound?"

"I like him. He keeps good company. I didn't say I love him."

"You might as well. If you keep seeing him that's exactly is what's going to happen."

"No matter what man I find to marry he will never be perfect."

"But he won't be a rapist."

"HE IS NOT A RAPIST. He is forgiven and that's what I believe. I knew you wouldn't understand."

"Then why did you come here?"

"Because you are all I have. My family refuses to talk to me about Bobby and refuses to accept him as their family. I haven't even told them about Sean and I know I cannot. You are all I have, William. You and Bobby is all the family I have left. I understand this is the most ridiculous situation, but I didn't create it. But, I don't find it too ridiculous to live it. I cannot change my past. I am not ashamed of Bobby, I am not ashamed of what happened to me, and I am not ashamed of Sean. It is what it is. I just want you to understand that. But most of all I really wish you can truly discover what forgiveness is. Because you are not so perfect that you can't give it. I'm sorry to bother you. I'll be leaving now."

"Don't go. I'm sorry. I get a little scared sometimes."

"Why? What is there to fear?"

"How does anyone explain this situation? I fear what people will think of me, of you, of us. This isn't the picket white fence family story."

"No one has the picket white fence family. And when you love someone; what someone else thinks should never matter to you. Those who care don't matter and those who matter don't care. Always remember that."

"Sarah."

"Yes, William."

"Do you really think its love?"

"I don't know. It could be infatuation, happiness, adoration, I don't know, but whatever it is, I've never felt it before."

"Well, regardless, do you think we can keep this quiet for now?"

"Who will I tell? You're all I have."

"Sarah, I'm sorry. I know commendation is wrong, but it's...so easy to do. But I guess if you can forgive him...there should be enough love in my heart to forgive him."

"Don't do it on my account."

Sarah thinks for a moment.

"Maybe you can meet him and see what kind of a man he is. I'm telling you; you'll never believe he could have done what he did."

"I don't know about that, Sarah."

"Think about it. I see him every Friday. Call me on Thursday and let me know. I'll see you later, William."

William gives Sarah a hug and then they say their good-byes.

Sarah and William are sitting quietly waiting for Sean. Soon a guard escorts Sean to the table. Sean looks surprised not aware who the man is. Both Sarah and William stand when Sean arrives. Sarah says, "Sean, this is William, Bobby's dad. William, this is Sean, Bobby's father. Well, that introduction sounded awkward."

As she introduces them they go to shake hands as they due the guard interrupts, "No touching."

William says, "Sorry, officer."

`They sit. There is a silence before Sarah breaks it, "Uh, Sean I thought that William should get to know you being that I visit you. I also wanted him to realize you are not the same person you were back when you, well, you know."

"Do I need to prove myself to him? Because I won't do that."

Sarah says, "No. it's nothing like that, it's just--"

William interrupts, "I will be honest with you Sean; I didn't like it at all when Sarah told me she was visiting you. I thought she was nuts. But she seems to see the good in you; so if she can, I can do the same. I've been thinking. Sarah and I have agreed on telling Bobby the truth on his sixteenth birth anniversary. I didn't know it at the time we made this agreement that she was seeing you, but being that she is; if Bobby decides he wants to visit you; are you up for that?"

"Well, I don't know. I never thought that I would get to see him."

Sarah interjects, "I think that would be a great idea."

Sean says, "I don't know."

Sarah is firm. "Why not?"

"What do I say to him? I don't want him looking at me after what I did."

"But you have forgiven yourself. Remember we talked about that?"

"But what if he doesn't forgive me. I couldn't take that. I mean, how do I explain to my son why I raped you?"

Sarah answers, "Tell him the truth."

"What if he doesn't care? What if he still doesn't forgive me? I really don't think I can look at him. Especially knowing he will know what I did. I cannot face that."

William speaks. "Well, we have another four years before we actually tell him so that will give you the time to strengthen your courage to face him."

Sarah agrees. "Exactly. Besides, I have to face him too you know. It's not going to be easy for me to tell him. Not to mention he thinks I'm William's friend and nothing more. To have to tell him who I am…we both will have to strengthen our courage. But don't worry because we can do it. All things are truly possible."

Sean thinks a moment. "Well, maybe you're right. In four years I'll think about it. Hopefully by then I will have the courage to face him."

William says, "Well, I'll tell you one thing. You'll know it's him because he looks *exactly* like you."

They all laugh. William continues, "You won't believe your eyes when you see him."

Sean says, "Thanks to Sarah I've seen him already. She brings me pictures of him all the time. He is so beautiful."

Sean begins to cry. "I don't know if I can look into those eyes and speak to him. It'll be like looking at me when I was a child. I can't face him."

William says, "Who? Bobby or Sean?"

Sean puts his head down in shame and cries even the more. Tears are dropping onto the table.

William speaks. "Sarah told me your story on the way here. I am so sorry for what happened to you, but if you do not deal with the child that's in you; you will never forgive yourself. You need to write a letter to your younger self, an apology letter. And when you do you need to forgive him and know that he will forgive you. There's no more shame, man. You have to let that go."

Sarah adds, "Sean, you need to deal with that boy who got abused. When you do; the shame will go away. I know it did for me."

The guard interrupts, "Times up."

Sarah says, "Well, we have to go, but don't forget about what we said. I'll be back next week."

William says, "I won't be able to come back with Sarah, but I will come back to see you. And I will ask the guards if I can bring you some tapes from my church. The messages will help you help that boy. Keep loving you, okay?"

Sean answers, "Yeah. Thank you, man. I really appreciate it. I wish I could hug you. I really need one."

William responds, "Well, when you get out I will make sure I give you a hug."

"Thanks, man. I appreciate it."

William says, "Well, Sean, see you soon."

Sarah says, "See ya, Sean."

They say their good-byes as the guard escorts Sean. Sarah and William soon leave after.

CHAPTER FIVE

William's door to his house opens and William, Bobby, Richard, Carla, and Ritchie enter the room. Richard speaks, "Goodness, Bobby, you keep this up you might be the youngest pro baseball player in the world."

William responds, "He did play a good game today. You made the parents of the other team mad."

Bobby speaks, "Dad may Ritchie and I go upstairs and play my new game?"

William answers, "If his parents say its okay, its okay with me."

Clara says, "Just for a little while; it's late."

Ritchie responds, "Thank you, William; thank you, Mom."

Bobby follows. "Thank you, Mrs. Clara, thank you, Dad."

Bobby and Ritchie run upstairs.

William responds,

"Walk, please."

William asks, "Can I get you guys anything?"

Richard asks, "You got a beer?"

Carla responds, "Richard, it's late."

Richard says, "Carla, may I remind you that my mother lives in Florida."

Carla says, "I'm just saying, it isn't good to drink alcohol this late at night."

Richard responds, "It's not that late."

William asks, "So, may I give him the beer or not?"

Richard sarcastically asks Carla, "Please, Mommy."
Carla responds,

"Oh, stop it. Go ahead."

William hands him the beer.

"Did you want something, Carla?"

Carla asks, "You got any hot tea?"

Richard interrupts, "Hot tea at this time of night?"

Carla responds, "Oh, come off it. I'll just have some tea, if you have it, William."

William responds, "I'll set the pot. Here are the tea bags."

Carla responds,

"Thank you, William."

Richard speaks,

"Well, can you believe our boys are growing up so quickly? I remember when we first met you and your boy. I think they were ten years old. Can you believe they're turning thirteen in a couple of months?"

Carla responds, "I know. They're going to be men soon. I don't know if I can handle that."

Richard asks, "Ritchie is planning a shindig for his thirteenth party. Is Bobby having a party?"

William answers, "Yeah. Ritchie didn't tell you? He's having a Bar Mitzvah."

Carla responds, "A Bar Mitzvah? What were you doing celebrating Christmas if you're Jewish?"

William answers, "I'm not Jewish."

Richard says, "Oh, his parents were Jews?"

William answers, "No. I mean, I don't know. He was invited to a Bar Mitzvah; some boy from his class. He liked it so much that he decided to have one. He's been doing the research and said that a Bar Mitzvah really is for anyone Jew or Gentile."

Richard responds, "Really? Well, ain't that something."

William adds, "You should be getting the invitations soon. He really has been working on it. How's your tea?"

"It's good, thanks. Ritchie is having a baseball themed party, of course. I cannot believe my boy is not my baby anymore. It seems only like yesterday when I was changing his diapers. Where did the time go?"

William answers, "I don't know. I only had him for three years and it seems like I had him forever. It is so weird how life happens. I never had any intentions on adopting a child and look at me; I'm a proud father."

Carla asks, "Speaking of which; how's it going at the office?"

"It's funny you ask. Just yesterday I officially gave my letter of resignation."

Richard asks, "Really? Has it been that bad?"

William laughs. "No, it's not that. I just want to spend more time on my business."

Carla inquires, "Oh, you have your own business?"

"Yeah, I had it for about seven years now. I started it a while ago. After getting hired at Bambin Adoption and Foster Agency I was able the make the money I needed to invest and market it."

Richard asks, "What type of business is it?"

"You see the artwork on my walls?"

Carla says, "Yes."

"I created them. They are all my original work."

Carla and Richard respond with shock. Carla says, "You are really good. They look like something you can buy at an art gallery."

"You will be able to soon. Right now I have all my work on sale on my website, but I have five shows coming up."

Carla responds,

"Really? Where at?"

William takes a flyer from off the refrigerator and hands it to Carla.

"You can keep that. I have plenty more. There's two here in Jersey, then two in New York, and one in Pennsylvania."

Carla says, "This is amazing. I'm really proud of you."

"Thank you."

Richard says, "I'm proud of you too, man. I didn't know you are an artist. We got a celebrity in our midst."

"I'm not a celebrity."

Richard says, "Oh, you will be. You create great art."

"Thank you."

Carla speaks. "Well, I think it's time for us to go. It's getting late."

Richard speaks. "Yeah. I gotta get up really early in the morning. I want to make sure I catch the horse races."

Carla says, "Oh, please, Richard. And I know one thing, you better not be gambling."

Richard responds, "Yes, mommy."

Carla says, "Oh, come off it."

They exit the kitchen and walk towards the door. Carla yells at the stairs,

"Ritchie, dear, its time to get going. You can see Bobby in the morning. Thanks for your hospitality William and good luck with your art shows. We will definitely come to at least one of them."

"No problem and thank you."

Bobby and Ritchie walk down the stairs.

Carla says, "See you later, Bobby. Ya'll have a good night."

They each say good night to each other. Carla, Richard, and Ritchie exit the house. Bobby then says goodnight to William gives him a hug and kiss and then goes back upstairs.

William smiles and says to himself, "I am really a father. This is something else."

There is a knock on the door of William's house. He gets up from his desk and walks to the door. He opens the door to see Sarah. "Hey, is everything okay?"

Sarah answers, "Yes. May we talk?"

"Of course, come right in. Is everything okay?"

"I don't know."

A silence hits the room as Sarah tries to speak. William asks, "What is it?"

Sarah looks him in the eyes. "He got early release. He gets out in six months."

"Oh, you mean Sean?"

"Yeah."

William confusingly asks, "Well, isn't this a good thing or not?"

"I guess. He has no where to go. He wants to live with me until he gets on his feet."

"That does not sound good."

"I know. I told him that, but he has no where to go. And I know he can't stay with you."

"Absolutely not."

"Do you have any suggestions?"

"Well, they have housing services for the poor or he can go to a shelter. I do not think he should live with you."

"Okay, that sounds good. I can tell him that the next time I see him. Do you still visit him?"

"Yes. And I am surprise he did not tell me."

"He just found out. He found a lawyer who volunteers his services for those in need. But I think all the prayer he and I have been doing finally worked."

"You don't plan to be with him?"

"I don't know. I thought about it and I really do not know. As you said I will let tomorrow take care of tomorrow."

"You're not going to bring him around?"

Sarah interrupts, "No, of course not. Anyone who sees him will know right away. I don't want anyone guessing anything. I want Bobby to be the first to know. I don't want him hearing anything through the grapevine."

"Well, until he's out, I guess we have nothing to think about. We will let the next six months take care of itself. I am sure all that is supposed to happen will and anything that is not; won't."

"Yes. Well, I'll see you later. Thanks for the chat. I appreciate you."

"You're welcome."

Time is passing by. Ritchie and Bobby have celebrated their thirteenth birth anniversaries, they are both preparing for high school, William has had a few more successful art gallery shows in the tri-state area, and what seems like a far time away has swiftly appeared. William, Sarah, and Sean are preparing for Sean's release; all are worrying about the truth finally coming into the light.

There is a knock on the door; William answers it. "Come in."

Sarah walks in the door. "Hello, William."

"Hey, Sarah."

They embrace. William continues. "So what brings you here?"

She is silent for a moment. William responds, "Is everything okay?"

"Yes. Everything is fine. I just needed to speak with you about Sean."

"Is he okay?"

"Yes, he is just fine."

"By the way, Sarah. You never actually told me the exact release date for Sean. I know a few months ago you said six months, but you never gave me an exact date. I would like to be ready, you know, mentally. You know, just in case we have to break the news to Bobby before he is sixteen."

"Well, that's what I came here to speak with you about."

"Oh, great. So when is he being released?"

"Well, the thing is--"

"Is he okay? He is being released, correct?"

"Well, sort of--"

"What do you mean sort of?"

"Well, you see--"

"Spit it out!"

"I'm trying, this isn't easy."

"Just give me the date!"

"Three weeks ago."

"WHAT? Three weeks ago? What are you talking about?"

"I was going to tell you, but I didn't think you would be okay with it. He had no where to go so I let him stay with me."

"Do you think that is wise? What happens if you get raped again?"

"He's not like that anymore. He really is a changed man. Besides I can't just leave him out on the streets."

William responds,

"There are homeless shelters and low income housing and there are other options as well."

"Well, this is the option I chose, okay. I am sorry, but I am doing my best to go with my heart. I know it may seem completely stupid, but this is what I feel is the right thing to do. He is kind and gentle and we have had no problems since he's been with me. You have to give him a chance."

"I just don't want to see you get hurt. He's been in prison for a long time. How do you know he is not conning you?"

"You know, William, I don't know. If this is a mistake then I will just have to find out, won't I? I know this doesn't seem wise, but I'm doing it, I'm already in it, and I will just have to see down the road whether this is a mistake or the right thing to do. We will both just have to wait and see."

There is a pause between them. Soon William breaks it. "Well, does he…does he…you know…does he go out a lot?"

"Well, sort of."

"What do you mean?"

"You know that store on Isabella Street that opened
Up about a year ago?"

"Yeah, Storecee."

"Well, he works there."

"He got a job already? How did he do that, he just got
out of jail?"

"The prison has a program. They have a list of all the
businesses in Jersey, New York, and Pennsylvania that hires
you regardless of your record or educational background.
Storecee just so happened to be on the list. He applied and got
the job a day later."

"Well, that seems odd."

"I think its God giving him a second chance. Sean
knows what he did was wrong. He apologized to me a hundred
times. He was messed up. He sought help and he's dealing
with his past. God forgave him I don't see why you can't."

"I forgave him, but it doesn't mean I have to trust
him."

"Well, I trust him. Okay. It is what it is. If I am an idiot, well, then I will find out soon enough. But as for now he is here and out of the house and on the streets and as you said what ever happens tomorrow it will happen. Let tomorrow take care of tomorrow. I am not going to worry anymore."

"Well, you seem pretty set in your ways. I guess there is nothing much I can do. Just so you know I am in disagreement with you, but I guess that means we have to agree to disagree. I truly hope all goes well with you and Sean. I pray the best for you two."

"Well, I thank you for your support."

She hands William a piece a paper. William asks, "What's this?"

"That is Sean's working hours. If you decide to go shopping in that store just make sure its not when Sean is working. Bobby is too smart for him not to figure out that is his father."

"Well, thank you. That was considerate of you. I appreciate that."

160

"You're welcome. Thank you for your support regardless of you disagreeing with me it means a lot to me. You are a true friend. I don't think I have ever had someone in my life as loyal and supportive as you. I really appreciate you." She embraces him. He returns the hug.

Sarah says, "Thank you, William."

"You're welcome, Sarah."

"Well, let me leave so you can get back to work. Thanks again, William."

Sarah walks towards the door opens it and then looks back and smiles, she then leaves the office. William sighs hard and then sits. He looks up and says, "Lord, if she is making a mistake please fix it. I thank you and appreciate it in advanced, Amen."

WILLIAM'S OFFICE—Three Days Later

William is about to leave for the day. As he does his final paperwork one of his co-workers enters his office.

"William, I am so sorry to disturb you. I need a huge favor."

"Nancy, what's wrong?"

"I have to go to the hospital. They just called, my husband passed out at work. They're not sure what's wrong yet."

"My gosh, I'm so sorry to hear that."

"Thank you. I have a client who is looking to adopt. They have some questions; I was wondering if you could take care of them for me."

"I have to pick up my son from Little League practice."

"Can't one of the parents do that for you? I'm sure you know someone from the league who can take care of your son for you. Please I have to go and they're in my office right now."

"Well, yeah, I guess. Let me give someone a call."

"Great. I'm going to send them over right away. Thank you, William."

She frantically leaves the office. William says as she leaves, "But, I haven't called them yet. I don't know if they'll be able to--. Goodness."

William sits at his desk picks up his phone and dials. "Hey, Carla, this is William."

"Hey, Will, what's going on? Oh by the way everyone is raving about your art that's hanging in my home. They just won't stop talking about it. I was thinking maybe you can have an art show in my home."

"That sounds good. Listen--"

"We can have refreshments: cheese, wine, chocolate--"

"Yes, I need you to--"

"We could have light jazz or classical music playing--"

"Great, can you--"

"We can even have a live band if you want. What do you think about that?"

"It's a great idea, but I need a favor from you."

"Oh sure, what is it?"

"An emergency popped up at work. I have to stay longer than I intended. Would you be able to pick up Bobby from baseball practice?"

"Well, of course. Is everything okay?"

"Well, yes. I have to cover for a co-worker. She had the emergency."

"That is not a problem. I'll pick him up and take the boys out to eat and they can hang out and when you get finished you can come over and pick him up."

"Carla, thank you so much. You are a life saver."

"What flavor?"

She laughs.

"Get it, what flavor? The candy?"

William gives a fake laugh and says, "Yes, I get it. That's real funny. Thanks again."

"Oh, no problem. Anything for a friend. You have a great day. See you soon."

"Okay thanks."

He hangs up the phone. Nancy comes in.

"William, this is Mr. and Mrs. Franco. This is the happy couple looking to adopt. Mr. and Mrs. Franco this is William Osei. He will answer any questions you have. I greatly apologize for leaving abruptly, but I have to go to the hospital."

Mr. Franco says, "It's not a problem at all. We understand."

Mrs. Franco chimes in, "Yes, please, go see about your husband. We will pray for him."

"Thank you. Bye William. And thank you."

"You're welcome."

Nancy rushes out of the office. William continues, "Well, Mr. and Mrs. Franco what questions may I answer?"

"The two of you are getting so much better at baseball. I know once you get into high school you're going to make the team. Oh, and wait until college. And I can't wait until you make the major leagues. Your dads are going to be so proud."

"Thank you, Mom."

"Thanks, Mrs. Carla."

"Oh no problem. So you boys hungry? What do you want for dinner?"

"Whatever you choose, Mom is fine for me."

"Really? What about you, Bobby, anything in particular?"

"No. I'm fine with anything."

"Well, alright. We'll stop by Elysia's Pizza Parlor. I hope you're not too hungry though, I want to stop by Storecee and get a greeting card and a little gift. We're having a going away party for a co-worker. I want to get it now before I forget. You guys don't mind, do you?"

"No, Mom. That's fine."

"Okay. I won't be long."

Carla, drives to the store and parks the car.

"You guys staying in the car or getting out?"

Ritchie asks Bobby, "You want to stay in or get out?"

"We can go in I guess."

Carla says, "Okay, let's go. I promise I won't be long."

They walk to the store. Carla goes in and goes to the greeting card section. The boys browse around. Soon the boys go their separate ways browsing the store. As Bobby browses he notices Sean, who is stocking shelves. He first notices his hair, but doesn't see his face. Shocked to see another person in the neighborhood with such bright red hair like his he gets curious.

As Sean turns around Bobby sees his face. Bobby then freezes. He stares at Sean not sure what to do or say. Confused he is not sure if Sean is a family member or a coincidence. During this time Sean does not notice him. Sean after some time walks back to the employee only door and enters it. Bobby then tries to walk back to the section, but as he does Carla speaks. "Bobby, you ready?"

Bobby taken off guard says, "What?"

"You ready to go? I told you I wasn't going to be long."

"Um…yeah, right. Yes. Uh-huh. I'm ready."

"Are you okay, Bobby?"

"Yes. Uh-huh. I'm fine."

"Okay, let's go."

CARLA AND RICHARD'S HOUSE

"Boys, I'll call you downstairs once William gets here, okay?"

"Yes, Mom."

"Okay, Mrs. Carla."

The boys go into Ritchie's room. Ritchie turns on the television and then takes the remote and begins to change the stations. Bobby stares at the television, but Ritchie can tell he is in outer space.

Ritchie calls him. "Bobby."

"Huh?"

"Is everything okay?"

"Yeah. Everything is fine."

"Are you sure?"

"Yes. Why are you asking me?"

"You seemed strange at the store."

"What do you mean?"

"You looked like you seen a ghost or something."

"Or something."

"What?"

"It's nothing."

"Bobby, what's wrong?"

"Ritchie, it's nothing."

"How long have we known each other?"

"Why are you asking?"

"Bobby, for the past three years we have been the best of friends. Don't you think that is long enough to trust me?

"What are you talking about, Ritchie? Why are you afraid to talk to me?"

"I'm not afraid to talk to you."

"Then what's wrong?"

"There is nothing wrong, Ritchie, okay. Just leave it alone."

"Okay, man, okay."

There is a brief silence before Ritchie breaks it.

"Well, when you're ready to talk I am ready to listen."

Bobby doesn't respond. He just stares at the television in a daze.

William and Bobby enter the house. As Bobby goes upstairs William stops him. "Hey. Is everything okay?"

"Yes."

"Are you sure? You were pretty quiet in the car. You look like you were thinking hard about something. Did you want to talk about it?"

"No, I'm good. I'm fine."

"Bobby, don't ever be afraid to talk to me, okay."

"I'm fine, Dad."

"You sure?"

"Yes."

Bobby proceeds to go upstairs and then pauses. William notices and asks,

"Are you okay, Bobby?"

"Dad, may I talk to you?"

"Of course. What is troubling you?"

Bobby walks towards the living room and sits. Confused William follows and sits next to him. Now worried, William wonders what could be the problem.

"Bobby, is everything okay?"

"Dad, I think I saw my dad today."

Knowing it is possible, William nervously says, "What? What do you mean?"

"I mean, I think I saw my birth dad."

"How? Where?"

"Mrs. Carla had to stop by Storecee today before we went to her house. I think I saw him there. There's a man that works there that looks exactly like me. Do you think it's a coincidence?"

"Well, all things are possible, you know. I mean I can't say that…what I mean is…you know maybe I can take you there tomorrow and you can show me. Maybe we can talk to him and find out."

"You would really do that?"

"Well, yeah."

"Dad, I'm scared."

"Son, me too."

They embrace. After the embrace William says, "How about you go upstairs and get some sleep. We'll talk about it some more tomorrow."

"Okay, Dad."

Bobby walks upstairs to his room. In the kitchen William picks up the phone and begins to dial. He then hangs up the phone and walks outside of his home and shuts the door. He takes out his cellular phone and dials. He then walks to his car gets in and shuts the door. Soon Sarah answers, "Hey, William. What's up?"

"We have a problem."

"What's wrong?"

"He saw him."

"What do you mean? What are you talking about?"

"He saw him. Bobby saw his father. Sean. Bobby saw Sean."

There is a slight pause before William breaks it,

"Sarah, are you still there?"

"Yes. How is that possible?"

"He was at the store."

"But I gave you his schedule so you wouldn't run into him. What were you doing there?"

"It wasn't me. I had an emergency at work and I asked Carla to pick him up and Carla stopped by the store and Bobby saw him...he saw him."

"Oh my gosh, this is not good. Well what did Sean say?"

"Well, I don't know. I don't know. Bobby didn't mention what he said; he just said he saw a man that looks like him. Oh my gosh, I don't know if Sean even noticed him. Is he there?"

"No he's still at work. What do we do? What the hell do we do?"

"Just calm down. We knew there was a chance this might happen. Just calm down. What did we prepare to do just in case this happened?"

"We didn't prepare anything yet. I gave you the schedule. I thought that would be enough so he wouldn't see him."

"WE DIDN'T PREPARE ANYTHING?"

"STOP YELLING!"

"I'm sorry; I am so sorry. I'm nervous, I'm scared, and I don't know what to do. I am not ready to tell him."

"I will never be ready to tell him, but we can't just ignore it. I mean if he told you he saw him you cannot just ignore it. He's going to find out eventually."

"This is all your fault."

"What are you talking about?"

"You should have told him to move to another state so there was never a chance Bobby would see him."

"This is not the time to play the blame game. There is nothing we can do now to change this. He saw his father and now the only thing we can do is go with it. It's here William, the day is here. It's not when we wanted, but its here. It's time to tell him."

"He is too young."

"If you tell him at sixteen he may never forgive you for lying to him all those years. I don't ever want to tell him, but he is eventually going to find out. That boy is smart, he is wise. He will find out on his own. I much rather he hear from us than anyone else. It's time William, it's time."

There is a silence amongst them. William wants to speak, but doesn't know what to say. Sarah breaks the silence.

"It's time, William."

William is sitting at his desk painting. Bobby enters the house.

"Hey, Dad."

"Hi."

Bobby runs upstairs and throws his book-bag on his bed he then runs downstairs frantically.

"I'm ready to go, Dad."

"Where?"

"To the store."

"What store?"

"Storecee. You said you would take me there today to find that man and ask him if he's my dad or at least related to me."

"Oh, sorry, son. We won't be doing that today."

"Why not?"

"Not today, son. Maybe another day."

"Maybe? But you said--"

"I know what I said, but not today."

"Why not? I want to see him?"

"Why?"

"Because it's not everyday you go into a store and see a man who looks exactly like you. Same hair, same eyes, same face. I want to know if he's a part of me."

"I understand, but not today."

"Why not!"

"You don't raise your voice at me. I said no!"

"I HATE YOU!"

Bobby runs upstairs to his room and slams the door. William sighs hard. He stands and then walks to the kitchen. He takes the phone and calls Sarah. Sarah answers, "Yes."

"Hey."

"Hi, William. Everything okay?"

"I need to speak with you."

"I'm listening."

William and Sarah have a long talk. After an hour of discussion William hangs up the phone and gives out a big sigh. He looks up and speaks, "Lord, are you sure I can bear this?"

Two days have passed and Bobby is barely speaking to William. Bobby has realized that William will not be taking him to the store to see this man. On the third day Bobby returns home from school. He enters the house and William calls him. "Bobby, come here, please."

With great attitude, Bobby says, "What do you want?"

"Don't talk to me like that. Come in here, now."

Bobby enters the living room and to his surprise he sees William, Sean, and Sarah.

"Hi, Ms. Sarah."

Sarah says, "Hello, Bobby."

"What are you doing here?"

"William is about to explain that."

"Daddy, that's the man."

William says, "I know."

"What do you mean you know?"

"Bobby, this is not going to be easy, but I need you to sit. I need to speak with you. We need to speak with you."

"Is he my father and why is Sarah here?"

"That's what we are here to speak with you about."

Sarah says, "Bobby, I don't want you to be angry, okay? Some times life doesn't happen perfectly. Sometimes life is so crazy that you have to just appreciate what you have not the bad things that have happened. And some times you have to be quick to forgive if you want to heal."

"Dad, what is she talking about?"

William says, "Sarah. I thought I was supposed to do all of the talking?"

Sarah says, "Sorry."

"Dad, what is going on?"

"Bobby, please sit down."

Bobby reluctantly sits.

"Thank you. Now, this is NOT going to be easy to say and I know it is not going to be easy for you to hear, but some times life is difficult like that."

"Dad, what is it?"

"Bobby, the man you see, his name is Sean. And yes, he is your father."

Bobby doesn't speak. He just stares at the man and suddenly tears fall from his eyes like water from a fountain. As Sean sees his son crying he freely begins to cry with him. As Bobby stares at him Sean whispers, "I'm sorry."

William continues, "Bobby, I want to apologize ahead of time for lying to you or deceiving you in any way, but I didn't know how to tell you this at the time I first met her, but Sarah is your mother."

Bobby looks at Sarah in shock and despair.

Sarah says, "I am so sorry for not telling you up front, but I didn't know how."

"It's not that difficult. You just say hi, I'm your mother and I gave you up."

In this moment the whole room is crying. Sarah frantically says, "No, it's not like that. It's not like that at all. I didn't give you up. You were taken from me."

"By whom? Who had the right to take me?"

"I want to tell you, I really do, but I…I just don't have the strength."

Sarah looks at Sean. Sean tries to respond. "Bobby, I…I…did a horrible thing to your mother. But it was my past. I didn't plan for this to happen."

"You gave me up for adoption? Why would you do that?"

"I didn't do it. I didn't…"

"Then who? Who gave me up!?"

William intervenes,

"Bobby."

"WHAT?"

"Listen."

"I'm listening, Dad. I AM LISTENING, but no one is telling me anything."

Sean interrupts. "I'm sorry, Bobby. I took advantage of your mother. She didn't plan to get pregnant. It was by force."

There is a slight pause in the room. Bobby can barely say, "You raped her."

Another silence. Sarah's face is full of tears,

"I forgave him, Bobby. I forgive him. He is a changed man. So please do not look at him as a criminal or an evil person. He's a good man now."

"Is that why you gave me up, Sarah, you didn't want me reminding you of him?"

"I didn't give you up. I was married at the time. My ex-husband took you when I wasn't home and gave you up for adoption. I am so sorry you had to hear this. But I guess it's the inevitable. It was going to happen at some point. I just wish there was a different story I could tell you, but there just isn't any. I am so sorry. I am really sorry."

Before William speaks a pause hits the room. An uncomfortable silence that all are hoping to break. William speaks, "If you want, Bobby, you can go to your room and we can talk about this later."

Bobby says, "Why are they here?"

"Once you told me you saw Sean, I knew it was time to tell you the truth. There was no way I could keep it from you anymore."

"Were you ever going to tell me?"

"We were going to tell you on your sixteenth birth anniversary. We thought you'd be old enough to understand it then."

"Is this ever understandable?"

"No, I guess not, but we just thought…that…"
Sarah interrupts, "I am sorry, Bobby, but there really is no right time and good way of doing this. We just thought that now would be the best time."

Bobby asks Sarah, "Why did you come back for me now?"

"I've been looking for you for a long time. When I found you three year ago I asked William if I could be in your life. I loved you from the moment I had you. I never wanted to let you go. I never stopped loving you."

Bobby looks at Sean. "And why is he here?"

Sarah answers, "I went searching for him. I wanted him to know he had a son. He was released from prison a few weeks ago. Once your dad told me you had seen him I knew it was time to just tell you the truth. I really wish I could tell you something better, but this is all I have. It's not the fairytale family story, but it's all I have."

Bobby says, "Do you love me?"

Sarah responds, "You know I do."

"I was talking to Sean."

Sean stands there staring at Bobby. Sean begins to cry again, his tears are flowing like a waterfall.

He finally speaks. "I'm pretty sure I do. I don't know you, but I can tell just by looking in your eyes that you are my son. I hate the fact that I have to tell you what a horrible man I was and the horrible thing I did to your mother, but as I look at you and I hear all the great things you have done in school and on the baseball field...there is something inside of me telling me that I love you. I am so sorry for what I did to your mom and I am sorry that you were given up for adoption, and I am really sorry to hear how many families have given up on you, but I am very happy that William chose to take you and I am grateful that William loved you more than I could ever love you. I know you are angry and confused, but no matter how you look at this situation, you are loved. Don't ever forget that. You understand?"

"Yes, I know."

Bobby stands. "Dad, may I go to my room now?"

William says ,"Of course you can."

Bobby walks upstairs to his room and shuts his door quietly. Once he is in his room William says, "That was not easy, but I am glad it is over."

Sarah says, "I feel a load has been lifted."

Sarah wipes her face, William notices and says, "Oh look at my manners. Let me go get us some tissue."

William runs to the bathroom and gets a box of tissue and hands tissue out to Sarah and Sean. Sean says, "Thank you, William. Well, I guess we should leave now."

Sarah says, "Yeah. Thank you, William. Call me if you need anything."

"I sure will. I'll see you to the door."

Sarah and Sean leave the house. William walks up the stairs and knocks on Bobby's door. Bobby doesn't respond. William speaks to the door, knowing Bobby is listening.

"I'm sorry, son. I love you and don't you ever forget it.

If you need to talk, you know I am here to listen."

CHAPTER SIX

Two weeks have passed since the news was given to Bobby. William is in his dining room at the table with Sean, Sarah, Richard, and Carla. Ritchie and Bobby are in Bobby's room. They just broke the news to Carla and Richard. There is a silence at the table. William breaks it. "Well, I know this is difficult for you to hear, but I figured you were going to find out any ways and I thought it would be better if you heard it from me instead of the neighborhood gossip, so that's why I thought now would be the time to break the news. Now that Sean is here and I'm sure people might be talking."

Sarah continues, "And being that you are almost like an uncle and aunt to Bobby, you should know the truth."

There is still a silence.

Bobby continues, "So. Do you have any questions?"

Carla proceeds, "Well, you know…it's just that…wow, it's just a shocker, you know…you don't expect something like this to…you know what I mean…it's just, you know…yeah."

William says, "Yes, I understand. You're speechless. You don't have to say anything, but we wanted you to know, because Sarah and Sean are going to be in Bobby's life now and we didn't want you wondering why. And we know you may disagree with it, but we talked about it and discussed it with Bobby and he seems to be okay with it."

Richard asks, "It seems like you're asking us for approval."

William says, "Not exactly. We just wanted you to know since you are like family. And there are no secrets in family."

Richard replies, "Well, give us some time to marinate on this. It's going to take some time I am sure you can imagine. And even more time to trust Sean. However, if you all think this is a good idea as your family, we will do everything we can to understand. But please give us some time."

William says, "Of course. Not a problem."

Richard stands and then says, "Well, I guess we can go now."

William says, "Oh sure, of course. I'll see you to the door."

William walks Carla and Richard to the door. Richard calls for Ritchie. Ritchie and Bobby come downstairs. Richard, Carla, and Ritchie leave the house. As they leave Bobby goes back to his room. Williams responds to the moment. "Well, that wasn't as bad as I thought it was going to be."

Sarah says, "Yeah, they took it pretty well. I just hope they don't change their minds and stop visiting. I would hate for Bobby to lose a friend over this situation."

Sean asks, "Do you think they needed to know?"

William says, "Yes. Besides, if you want to be in Bobby's life there is no reason to keep it a secret. People are going to start asking questions. And yes it is none of their business, but the more lies you tell the more lies you have to remember. It is better to tell the truth and shame the devil. You are forgiven, Sean. That was your past. There is no reason to be ashamed or guilty."

Sean says, "Thank you, William."

"You're welcome."

Sarah and Sean leave. Once they are gone William calls for Bobby. Bobby opens his door and pops his head out.

"Yes, Dad."

William smiles at Bobby and with assurance says, "I know it seems impossible, but things are going to get better."

Bobby gives him a smirk of assurance and then says, "Thank you, Dad."

"Don't forget it."

"I won't."

Eight months have passed and Sean and Sarah have been seeing Bobby more often. With William they have been taking Bobby to museums, parks, movies, and many other entertaining places. Bobby is now getting used to the idea of his parents being in his life. Sean and Sarah have also been spending time with Richard and Carla. Richard and Carla have been more reluctant to accept them, but as time goes on they begin to accept Sean and Sarah. All of the relationships are slowly, but surely getting stronger and forgiveness is being sent to one another.

Sarah frantically enters.

William says, "Is everything okay? What brings you here?"

Sarah is pacing the floor. She looks up at William with tears in her eyes. Williams says, "What the hell is wrong with you? Did he hurt you? Did Sean hurt you? I told you; you couldn't trust him. Where is he? Did you call the police?"

"Stop it. He didn't hurt me."

"Then why are you crying"

"I am very confused."

"Confused about what?"

There is a silence in the room. Sarah, crying, trying to speak the words finally speaks. "I'm pregnant."

Another silence hits the room. William breaks the silence. "What do you mean?"

"I'm pregnant."

"By who?"

"Who do you think?"

William thinks for a moment then reacts,

"Did he rape you again?"

"No! I told you he is not like that. It was consensual."

William stares into space for a moment before coming to.

"You mean to tell me you and Sean..."

"I know. I don't understand it either. I told you I was confused...I think I love him."

William laughs,

"If this is some kind of joke it surely is a cruel joke."

"I wish it was a joke. I don't know what it is, but there is something about him."

"How can you be in love with him? How could you be in love with your rapist?"

"I DON'T KNOW. I have been trying to HATE him for what he did to me, but the more I try to hate him the deeper in love I get. It's just the things he does, the little things that make me so attracted to him. I mean he wakes up and makes me breakfast, when he comes home from work he cooks dinner and washes the dishes afterwards. He pays the cable bill, he leaves the toilet seat down, and he has a dream business that he works on instead of sitting around watching football like most men. He actually is a changed man. And I tried to hate him so I wouldn't notice how attracted I am to him, but it's not working. And one night one thing led to another and it was just so good. Not the sex, but being with him. I just couldn't stop."

"Well, how many times did you do it before you got pregnant?"

"I don't know I wasn't counting."

"Oh my gosh. When did it start?"

"About a month or two after we told Bobby the truth. Seeing him cry and talk to his son, that was the first thing that drew me to him. I kept thinking I cannot be in love with him. This is not how love is supposed to work. But through it all I have never loved; so I wouldn't even know if this is how it's supposed to work. My first husband I married out of low self-esteem. It wasn't love. So maybe, maybe this is how it's supposed to be for me, but it's got me so confused. I don't know what I should do."

"Well, I sure as hell don't know. Why are you telling me?"

"Because I need to tell someone and you are the only one I trust to talk to."

"Well, I'm flattered, but I haven't a clue of what to tell you. I mean I could never think anyone could be in love with someone who abused them, but…I don't know…Are you keeping the baby?"

"Of course! I could never give up a child."

"Well, how do you plan to tell Bobby about his little brother or sister?"

"I don't know. I haven't figured out how to tell his father yet."

"He doesn't know?"

"You're the first to know. Well, the third. The doctor was the first; I'm the second to know and now you."

"Well, actually I'm the fourth to know. God was the first."

Sarah laughs. "Yeah, I guess you're right."

There is a silence between the two of them before William breaks it. "This has been the wildest journey I have ever been on."

They both laugh.

Sarah is in the elevator talking to herself pretending she is talking to Sean trying her best to figure out how to tell Sean the news. There are two other individuals in the elevator staring at her like she is crazy. The elevator stops and Sarah walks off. She approaches her door and sighs heavily.

"You can do this Sarah. Just go in there and tell him. It's no big deal." Sarah unlocks the door and then opens it. As she enters she hears jazz music playing. With much shock she hesitates to walk in. As she does she calls for Sean. Sean answers,

"I'm in the dining room."

Sarah walks towards the dining room and sees the table set for two with candles. There is a gift box at one of the settings. Sarah begins to cry.

"What are you doing, Sean?"

Sean says, "Take a seat. I wanted to have dinner with you."

"This is amazing. You did this all for me?"

"Of course. And you deserve more. I wanted to thank you."

"Thank me for what?"

"Forgiving me. You didn't have to and yet you did. You'll be amazed at what forgiving someone can do for them. I appreciate it and do not take it for granted."

"Well, you're welcome."

"Please be seated."

As she seats Sean removes the chair from the table so she can sit once she is seated he helps her move the chair closer to the table, he then sits opposite of her. As she sits she notices the little gift box with the words Francine's Jewelry on the table next to her place setting. She replies to the box,

"What is this?"

"Open it."

"Sean, what is this?"

"Open it."

She takes a sigh and then takes the box and opens it. She notices the 14 Karat White Gold Pave Double Halo Engagement Ring with Pave Split Shank Design and begins to cry. She looks at him and asks again,

"What is this?"

Sean says, "I cannot see my life without you. And I do not want to keep being with you without you being my wife. I really did try to believe I could go on by myself, but I just cannot see it. It may sound crazy considering what I have done to you in the past, but I really like you, I admire you, I appreciate you, and I love you. I do not know if you feel the same way, but I thought I let you know how I feel about you. Lastly, I really enjoy the time we spend together with Bobby and was hoping maybe we could have another child together. Now I know it sounds crazy and abnormal, but I don't care about being normal. I really believe we belong together. Now if you are uncomfortable with that let me know and I will move out as soon as I can and never mention it again."

There is a silence that hits the room hard. Sarah does her best to speak, but cannot find the words to express herself at the moment. Sean breaks the silence, "If you need time to think about it let me know. All I need is a yes or a no."

Sarah finally breaks through her tears and says, "I'm pregnant."

"WHAT?"

"I'm pregnant."

"Oh my goodness! Really?"

Sarah nods her head yes. Sean continues,

"Well, that's great! Well, is that a yes or a no?"

Sarah takes the ring and puts it on her finger and then answers, "Yes. Yes, I will marry you."

Sean embraces her. They then kiss passionately.

SAMUEL AND ELIZABETH'S DINER

Two weeks later. Sean and Sarah are sitting at a table waiting patiently. Soon William comes rushing in. He speaks to the host and the host leads William to the table Sean and Sarah are sitting at. William speaks, "So sorry I am late. I had a meeting today about an art show. It ran later than I expected."

Sean says, "We completely understand. Thank you for coming."

William says, "No problem. So is this just a date or is there a specific reason why we are meeting here?"

Sarah says, "Well, we wanted to tell you something and we thought it should be outside of your home."

Sean continues, "Yes, we thought you should know before we tell anyone else including Bobby."

William asks, "Is everything okay?"

The waitress interrupts and the three of them order their drinks and meals once she leaves William continues, "Okay, so where were we?"

Sean says, "Well, as weird as this may sound."

Sarah continues, "And we already know how weird it sounds-"

Sean continues,

"But, we have decided to get; well we wanted you to know that we are getting-"

William interrupts them,

"Getting what? Just spit it out, man."

Sean continues, "Well, the thing is-"

Sarah holds her hand up and shows William her engagement ring. William with much shock grabs her hand and looks at the ring. He then asks, "Is that what I think it is?"

Sean answers, "Well, if you think it's an engagement ring then yes. We're getting married."

William says, "Oh. Is it because Sarah's pregnant?"

Sarah says, "No. He asked me to marry him before I had the chance to tell him I was pregnant. That's why we believe it was meant to be. I am not sure if we are making a mistake, but if it is a mistake we are willing to make this mistake together."

William responds, "This is so...I can't even because...like what is...sorry, but I am so lost for words."

Sean replies, "Well, hold off on your words because that's not all we have to say."

"What more is there to say?"

Sean says, "Well, I was wondering if you wouldn't mind being my best man. I really don't have anyone in my life. You have been the best thing to me, Sarah, and our son and I want you to be at my side when I get married."

"Wow. Yeah, I don't know what to say other than...wow."

Sarah continues. "There's one last thing. As you know I'm pregnant and being that you are Bobby's legal father we were hoping that you would be our baby's Godfather. We couldn't think of anyone else other than you who we would be honored to ask."

Sean continues. "Now I know we put a heavy load on you so we don't mind if you take some time to think about it."

Sarah says, "We're setting the date and making the arrangements so once it's set we are going to need an answer. And you have less than nine months to make decision about the being the Godfather of William, Jr."

William says, "You're naming the baby after me?"

Sean says, "If you don't mind."

William asks, "What if it's a girl?"

Sarah says, "We will name her Liam."

William says, "You have me speechless. I don't even know what to say, think, or do right now."

The waitress arrives with their meals. Once she leaves Sarah says, "Well, I guess you can just eat. Pray about it and when you have an answer let us know. There's no rush. And one last thing."

William asks, "And what is that?"

Sarah says, "Thank you for everything. You have been met with the strangest situations concerning me and my life and you have done nothing but love me through it. Thank you for taking care of Bobby, thank you for allowing me into his life and thank you for trusting Sean; I know that wasn't easy."

Sean chimes in, "You have really demonstrated the love of Christ. I greatly appreciate you."

William sits there in tears not knowing what to say he just takes his fork and eats. Sean and Sarah smile at him and begin their feast as well. They finish their meals and William promises to give them an answer before the month is out. They greet each other and leave.

CHAPTER SEVEN

Time goes by so quickly when you are having fun. Three years have passed and Sean and Sarah are husband and wife and their son William, Jr. is two years of age and Bobby is sixteen. Every Friday night they take their son Bobby and spend time with him. They have been doing this for the past three years. On Sunday they return Bobby to William. During the summer Bobby gets to stay with them for the month of July and parts of August. It's an arrangement Bobby, William, Sean, and Sarah agreed to after Sean and Sarah's marriage became final. Bobby as always returns home from a weekend with his parents on a cold February day. He enters William's home and goes straight to William. William notices him.

"Hey, son. How did things go?"

"Everything went well."

William looks at Bobby strangely and then asks, "What's on your mind? I can tell when you need to talk."

"You won't be upset with me will you?"

"Bobby, what did you do?"

"Nothing. I wanted to talk to you about something."

"I'm listening."

"When I was a child back in those foster homes I would always imagine my parents coming back for me and taking me home. A part of me thought that it could never happen, but then there was a part of me that had always had the faith to believe indeed it could happen. So the fact that I get to be with my parents it's just amazing. And although the circumstances of how I got here are not good; to see my parents get along despite…it just makes me happy."

"Well, I am happy for you. I am glad your dreams came true."

"The thing is my dreams weren't me spending the weekend with them. Now, I know I am pretty older now and I only have a couple of more years at home, but I was wondering if I could spend them with my parents. I thought that maybe I could spend my last year of high school living with my parents. It's not that I don't appreciate you, but all I ever wanted was for them to return to me and they have. And now before it's too late I want to be able to come home from school to them. I want to see them at the dinner table and be able to live with my brother and be with him like a family is supposed to. I want to live like a normal family even though my family is not normal. I hope you can understand without being offended."

William says, "What do your parents think? Are they okay with you moving in with them?"

"I haven't asked them yet. I figured I should ask you first."

"Well, I am a bit saddened to see you go. I raised you since you were ten. This of course won't be easy for me, but in everything I did for you I simply wanted you to be okay. And if this is what you need; to be okay; then I am okay with it."

Bobby grabs William and embraces him with a hug. "Thank you, Dad. I love you."

"I love you more."

They embrace again.

THE HOUSE OF SEAN AND SARAH

Sean, William, and Bobby are casually talking. They are waiting Sarah's arrival. Once Sarah enters the living room William speaks, "Well, here she is."

"I am so sorry. Sometimes he fights his nap so hard it takes so long just for me to get him to sleep."

"And how is my Godson doing?"

Sarah says, "He is doing just fine. But he is a handful."

Sean says, "Yes he is, but I love him. He is the second miracle of this family."

Bobby says, "Who would be the first?"

Sean answers, "You, Bobby. You are our miracle."

Sarah continues, "Yes you are. So what brings you two here?"

William answers, "Well, Bobby needed to speak with you and I came for support. Before he begins allow me to say I am in agreement and I have given my consent."

Sean asks, "Oh, well, what is it, Bobby? What did you need to say?"

Bobby begins, "Well, actually, I came here more so for a request."

Sarah asks, "A request, what kind of a request?"

Bobby continues, "Well, I've been thinking about my past and my future and I realized there was something I have always wanted. I also realize if I don't get it now I may never get it. Before William took me in I was shipped from one foster house to another. They always ended up sending me back saying they didn't want me. Every night before going to bed I would pray and ask for my real parents to come back and get me. Once William took me I figured that was good enough. He really took good care of me. But then when you both showed up out of the blue I got the thinking again of how I always wanted to be with you. I only have a year left before I leave for college and live on my own and so I was wondering if you wouldn't mind me living out that last year with you. Like a family."

Sean and Sarah shocked and amazed at the request sit speechless. Bobby continues, "If the answer is no I completely understand. I'm not a child anymore so having me live here would be kind of weird and all, but I thought that maybe we could somehow be a family again."

Sean speaks, "You trust us like that?"

Bobby says, "I don't know. But I know that I love you. And I know I want to give this a try. I mean, if it doesn't work out I can always go back to dad, but I don't want to give up on this hope. This is the last chance I have of making my dreams come true. I have this chance it's right in front of me and I do not want to pass it up."

Sarah speaks "I am willing to give it a try."

Sean says, "Me too. If your father is okay with this then yes, you can move in."

Bobby's face is filled with tears. "Thank you."

Sean stands and grabs Bobby. They share a hug. Sarah stands and hugs Bobby once Sean has let go. William hugs Bobby last and then speaks, "Well, I guess this is good bye for me."

Bobby speaks. "Dad, it's not good bye, its see you later. You know I'll come visit you."

Sean says, "Well, if you want I can go back with you to help you pack."

William says, "We packed already. Everything is in the car."

Sarah says, "How did you know we were going to say yes?"

Bobby says, "I was walking by faith."

Sean says, "Well, let's go. I'll help you take everything out."

William, Sean, and Bobby leave the house and get Bobby's belongings and bring them into the house. Once everything is in the house William gives Bobby a huge hug and then greets Sean and Sarah with a hug good bye and leaves.

Bobby makes the decision to legally change his name to Murphy. They spend the next two years together before Bobby leaves for trade school.

A year after Bobby left; William met his future wife, Ruth and two years later they were married. Of course so much more has happened, but there is never enough time to put it in a book so the rest is left up to your imagination.

If you haven't learned anything from this book always remember that forgiveness is powerful.

FOR MORE INFORMATION ON BOOKS BY

CASEY BELL VISIT HIS WEBSITES

http://authorcaseybell.weebly.com/

http://payhip.com/caseysbell

Thanks to my Editor: Michael Valentine
http://editor-ghostwriter.com/

 bookcasepublishing.weebly.com